L. RIFKIN
THE NINE LIVES OF
Romeo Crumb

LIFE TWO

Stratford Road
Press, Ltd.

Library of Congress Control Number: 2005930646

ISBN 0-9743221-6-4

Printed in the United States of America.
First edition, 2005.

THE NINE LIVES OF
Romeo Crumb

Illustrations by Kurt Hartman

LIFE TWO

Chapter One

It was getting colder as evening set in. The faint, wet wind whistled and howled through the cracks in the Factory walls on East 54th Street as the last few candles dripped hot wax to the floor. Outside, a thunderous storm dumped massive buckets of water all over the city. Upstairs, Romeo had awakened from his first death, but had immediately fallen back into a deep and sound sleep. He lay still on two covered, metal lunchboxes, an old t-shirt draped over his body. His breath left his mouth in tiny, smoky clouds along with a slight wheezing sound. Underneath the thin, cotton shirt even his bloodiest wounds from Fidel's rampage had healed and disappeared as they do after a death. Old Mr. Sox sat by his side in the musty medicine room as he waited for Romeo to come to again. While he sat watching Romeo begin to twitch,

Chapter One

frightening visions of war and revenge swirled through his aged mind, all directed at Fidel and his evil, violent ways.

Down in the rec room, usually a place of enjoyment, the mood was grave. Everyone was too nervous to talk. They were scared. Scared of Fidel, leader of the Alley cats, and his power over them. Scared of more attacks and lost hope. Scared just to be scared. They sat quietly on pillows and listened to the rain tap against the walls, waiting, wondering. It was to be such a happy day for the Sticks, *Stick* being the name for the domes*tic*, or homebound cats in the city. Graduation from Stick School was always a big event for the proud graduates who had worked so hard in the classroom. Learning to read, write, and survive meant a lot to the life-hungry cats. As for the people of the city, they never knew such a place even existed. The Stick School was located in the Factory, an old worn out umbrella factory that the Sticks took over as their one haven outside home. The Alleys *supposedly* wouldn't bother them there.

No one could fathom why Fidel and the rest of the Alleys had to go and ruin the big day. Never before had such a bloody scene taken place, at least none that anybody could remember. Not only was it bad enough that little six-month old Romeo lost his first life in the fight, or that beloved Queen Elizabeth, Romeo's mentor, sadly lost her ninth, but Fidel had taken away any fleeting hope that city life could once

Life Two

again be grand and carefree. Enraged, the Sticks were not going to forget so easily. Not this time. Fidel and the rest of the grisly Alleys were sure to pay for what they had done.

A startling voice echoed from the soup shaft. "He's awake! Romeo's awake!" Mr. Sox hollered, lowering himself in the soup pot, the Factory's own makeshift elevator. Although dented and worn, the cats were successful in creating quite a device, equipped with a sophisticated system of levers and pulleys to lift and lower them from floor to floor, just like a real elevator. Mr. Sox tugged and pulled frantically at the ropes using an unheard of amount of energy for such an old male. "Come quick!"

Everyone jumped from their spots and ran to Mr. Sox in a huff. They banged into each other as they rumbled toward the pot.

"Let me up there, Mr. Sox," Fluffy insisted in his pretty pink panties that Cassie, his person, had dressed him in. "I'm his best friend."

"I've got to see him!" Tabitha cried.

A crowd of about fifteen cats gathered around Mr. Sox, pleading with him to see Romeo. Even those who hardly knew him begged, intrigued by the fact he had been personally targeted by Fidel, a rare occurrence for a kitten. Octavian, the spider, watched the frenzied scene from the ceiling. He sucked the sweet blood from a fat fly as he peered over the rafters.

Chapter One

Mr. Sox lifted his glasses and balanced them on the edge of a wooden beam. "Let me see," he said with a squint. "I will take up five at a time. I don't want any crowds. Romeo needs his rest." He looked out among the innocent faces and wished that the whole tragedy had been a dream. It hadn't. "All right, now remember Romeo's had a hard day, a very hard day, far worse than the rest of us. So be kind to him. Don't ask him about Queen Elizabeth or Fidel. Just let him know you're here for him."

Mr. Sox pointed to Fluffy, Tabitha, Darla, dear, old, stupid Uncle Fred, and Twinkle Toes; Romeo's closest friends and ex-classmates. They would be the first to visit.

They all waited quietly at the soup pot for Darla who was urgently peeing in the corner of the photo lab. Unfortunately, Waldo, the Factory photographer, had left the door open. Darla ran in knowing she would never make it to the litter room. With a bladder like hers, it happened a lot. She peed on a bent photograph of Calvin, the Factory's very own actor. When Waldo returned from his walk, he would understandably be upset to find the stinging scent of urine staining his office. Darla finished and took a nervous look around, then joined her friends.

Mr. Sox allowed the females to climb into the pot first. He and Uncle Fred pulled the frayed ropes through the squeaky hinges as the pot rose to the third floor. Up, up they went, disappearing into the darkness.

4

Life Two

Outside the medicine room Mr. Sox brought everyone to a stop. He stood in front of the door and faced the five eager cats. Below him the rotting floor creaked and moaned like an old ghost. "Now remember," he began for the zillionth time, "Romeo has been through a harrowing ordeal. *Don't* ask him about it! Let me handle it." He gave everyone a stern look and pushed against the splintered bottom of the medicine room door. Fluffy looked at Darla and heaved a nervous sigh.

The door slowly opened. Tiny specks of light twinkled around the cats' heads, putting out an eerie, distorting glare on the far wall, the kind nightmares are made of. At the center of the small room lay Romeo, looking weak and tired and lifeless. His eyes were open, though deep and vacant. Behind him on a small counter were a bloody rag and some sharp, rusty tools. He looked like a corpse, eyes staring straight ahead without a single blink.

Mr. Sox led everyone in. They moved together as one lump deeper into the room each staring into Romeo's empty face. They gritted their teeth in anger and disgust as they remembered why he was on that table. Tabitha was the first to step closer. For a little thing she was strong, stronger than most thought. After all, it was she who saved Queen Elizabeth from the cat at the Pound, and it was she who risked a life to save Romeo from Fidel. Nervously, she positioned herself beside Romeo's battered body and sat on the dank floor.

5

Chapter One

Tabitha lifted her right paw and gently stroked Romeo's face. His little, white whiskers bounced and bent as her paw grazed over them. In her head she thought about the first time she met Romeo. It was at Stick School. As kittens go, he was as cute as they come; full of energy and life, a spark in the crowd. Those first few weeks together were the best. Climbing around the Factory searching for mice, playing after school. She would never forget those times and forever long for others like it. Now, as she sat beside the same young male she had played with, she wondered where that little kitten was. His once happy, carefree smile was already scarred with memories of tragedy and death.

Tears streamed down her cheeks as she turned to see her friends watching silently. Although the cats had been through a horrible day, she was grateful at least they were all still together, and hoped they always would be. This realization gave her the strength she needed to sit with Romeo in his moment of need and somehow overcome the sadness that had crept into their lives. After a long hesitation, Tabitha whispered, "Romeo. Romeo, it's...Tabitha. Do you remember me?" Looking down at him, she saw his breath moving swiftly throughout his body.

Suddenly, Romeo's eyes opened wider with a hint of recognition. He lifted his head slightly and gave her a long, curious stare. Then, he took in a short, sharp breath and groaned a painful meow. Tabitha smiled, "Oh, Romeo!" But just as she went to

Life Two

hug him, a blank expression fell upon his face, and he dropped his head. Tabitha stood back. Romeo twisted and turned his body until he was facing her and the others. She went to reach for him again, but Mr. Sox stuck out his paw to stop her. He shook his head *no* and motioned that she step away.

Relieved to have seen him, yet deeply saddened, they all stepped out of the medicine room and headed back downstairs.

Chapter Two

Romeo was drifting in and out of sleep, snoring and making bubbling noises with his mouth. His friends were carefully watching his every move in one-hour shifts. Finally, after several hours, Romeo spoke as Maybelle, a younger, Stick School alum, dozed off beside him. Sleepy Maybelle shot up on all fours at the sound of his voice.

"Queen Elizabeth," Romeo moaned with a cough. "Q-Q-Queen Elizabeth?"

Maybelle bent down closer to Romeo's face and whispered, "Romeo? Are you all right?" She placed her paw to his chest and gently rocked him.

"Queen Eliza-b-beth, oh no," Romeo mumbled again. Only this time as he spoke he began to weep.

"Wait here!" Maybelle sparkled as she darted toward the door. She grabbed onto the wall, taking one more quick glance at Romeo. Certain that he was safe, she sped to the rec room in search of Mr. Sox.

He was still there, though others had gone home in order to not worry their people. Those who stayed were passing the time rehashing the events of the day, the graduation ceremony at City Park, the attack by Fidel and his gang, the killing of Queen Elizabeth, and Romeo. Talk of a possible retaliation war was in the air. Some were thirsty for Alley guts and blood.

"He's up!" Maybelle shouted grinning whisker's end to whisker's end. "He keeps calling for Queen Elizabeth. I didn't know what to do."

Mr. Sox jumped out of his seat worried. "What did you say to him?"

"Nothing! I didn't know what to say. I came straight down here. Come on, let's go!" Maybelle waved her tail and headed back to the soup pot. Twinkle Toes, Mr. Sox, Darla, Soot, Vittles, Uncle Fred, and Fluffy followed.

Everyone rushed to get to the medicine room, making two trips in the soup pot. When they arrived, they found Romeo sitting up on the table. His fur was messy and his eyes red, but he was back. Mr. Sox went in first. "Romeo," he said smiling. "Romeo, you're okay, little one. You're going to be okay."

Romeo looked about the room at all of his friends, then quickly spotted the bloody rags around him. "Was it a dr-dr-dream? Please tell me it was all a dream. Is Queen Elizabeth r-r-really gone?" He whined, catching sight of Fluffy who nodded and frowned. Romeo's friends huddled nearby, but no one said a word. He cleared his throat and asked again, "W-w-where is she now? Her...body, I mean. She's not still out...*there,* is sh-she?"

"No, Romeo," Vittles answered. "Waffles and Roy got her. They brought her home, you know, were she lives....lived."

"Oh, p-p-poor Gwen, she's going to be heartbroken," Romeo sadly said. "Is...is she j-just laying there on the cold stoop?"

"Yes. What else could they do?" Vittles explained sympathetically.

Romeo looked down. "I g-guess you're right."

"Are you okay, Romeo? What's wrong with your voice?" Fluffy asked delicately.

Romeo circled the room with his puffy, blurry eyes. "I..I..I don't know. Is there s-s-something wr-wr-ong with my voice?"

"Never mind that," Mr. Sox quickly injected. "Stuttering's a very common reaction after you've lost... well, don't worry, it'll go away soon enough. It's just the body's defense against shock," Mr. Sox whispered. "Tell me, do you...remember anything, Romeo?"

"I can't, I c-can't!" Romeo wailed. "It's too awful!"

"You can do it, Romeo," Darla whispered. "We're all here."

Life Two

Romeo took a deep breath and let it exhale through his tiny, pink nose. His eyes squinted and dripped a few sad tears. "Well," he began, "I remember we were all at City P-park and Twinkle T-t-toes had just r-r-read that nice poem he wrote."

"Yep," Twinkle Toes beamed proudly.

"Then, I th-think the next thing that happened was...I heard a l-l-loud noise and Queen Elizabeth was s-s-screaming something! Everybody started running away," Romeo's heart began to pound as he recalled the events. "Yeah, then *they* sh-showed up, and they-they jumped on her. I heard her s-s-scream louder, but when I went over to her, it was too late. I saw b-blood everywhere!" Romeo covered his eyes with his paws. Mr. Sox patted him gently on the back. "F-F-F-Fidel was on top of me! His c-c-claws were so sharp, and I was so-so scared. I t-tried to run but he h-h-held me down. I couldn't breathe. That's when he told me about my b-brothers and my parents." Romeo's head drooped as he relayed the ghastly details that rang from Fidel's mouth; how he and his gang viciously killed Romeo's whole family just because they wanted to give up Alley life and become Sticks.

"Yes, Romeo," Mr. Sox said with a sigh. "What a terrible tragedy to lose one's parents and brothers all at the same time. But, you were lucky, he didn't get *you* that fateful day."

"Lucky? I don't know how l-lucky I am. He called me an *Alley*! Once an Alley, always an Alley!"

Chapter Two

Romeo sat up quick and straight, but flopped back down from a sudden sharp pinch in his back. His entire body was sore.

"Take it easy, man," Twinkle Toes suggested. "You just lost a life, dude. You don't wanna be moving around so fast. Listen, I won't tell anyone you're an Alley. Your secret's safe with us. God knows I'd never wanna be thought of as an Alley, no way."

"You're not helping! And he's not an Alley!" Mr. Sox snapped. He thought hard, then took a few steps around the medicine room and walked back to Romeo's side. "Now listen, Romeo," he began sternly. "You *are* lucky. Just look at all the faces around you."

Romeo's eyes circled the roomful of friends. They looked tired and worried, yet had remained steadfast by his side.

"And don't even think about all that *Alley* talk," Mr. Sox continued. "I know Fidel told you that since your parents were Alleys, *you* are an Alley too. You've been raised by Dennis, a human boy, and that makes you a *Stick* regardless of where your parents were from. Besides, many Sticks are rescued Alleys, so *don't* let Fidel make you believe you're something you are not. In your chest beats the heart of a Stick. Your good parents knew that, so should you. So, are you going to believe Fidel or me?" Mr. Sox walked away angry that Fidel had power over Romeo even when he was nowhere in sight, and headed for the door. He was far too old for this day.

Life Two

"Wait Mr. S-Sox," Romeo called. Mr. Sox stood in the doorway with his bent tail to Romeo. "I'm s-sorry, I'm sorry," the kitten sobbed. "I just w-w-want to go home."

Mr. Sox turned and headed back to Romeo. He looked him over, then at the others. "Okay," he said in a whisper. "Then let's go home."

Uncle Fred helped Romeo down from the table and out the door. Everyone gave him a boost into the soup pot. Soot threw away the bloody rag then turned off the flashlight in the medicine room. Ever vigilant, Vittles stayed behind to begin his night shift at the entrance. He was ready to take on anyone who got in his way. Waffles had been on guard duty all afternoon and was exhausted and hungry. Soon, everyone went separate ways, except Maybelle, who volunteered to walk Romeo home.

"I've never seen it rain so hard," she squealed as she darted from awning to awning, her pretty red and gold fur soaked to the roots. "I think it's actually raining mud. This El Queso thing is too much!"

Romeo agreed. Still, he stayed quiet and walked with his head to the wet ground. He prayed that Fidel wasn't out there, lurking around, waiting to pounce. He was still so paranoid he could hardly breathe. Maybelle, who was a little less scared and a little more naive, bounced around playfully, following a lost fly. She was about to snatch him when a huge raindrop fell from a street lamp and smacked the fly to the ground and into the gutter. Down he went far into the sewer, choking and drowning in the filthy water.

"Drat!" Maybelle stomped, watching the tasty morsel float out of sight.

Eventually, the two cats reached Romeo's building. They both took a long, difficult glance toward Queen Elizabeth's old apartment standing grey and tall as the brutal weather crashed against it. Romeo and Maybelle squinted through the heavy downpour. On the doormat was a small pile of leaves, but no cat. They looked at each other as their stomachs started to churn.

"That must be where she w-w-was," Romeo said in low drone. "P-p-poor Gwen."

"Yeah," Maybelle sighed. "Well, I guess we better get going, Romeo. But listen, you're home now, and everything's going to be fine." She said it, though she didn't sound convinced. "Now, I hope to see you at the Factory tomorrow, okay?" She nudged him with her nose.

Romeo nodded his head though the thought of tomorrow was a world away. He felt like staying inside for the rest of his lives and never going out again.

"Be careful!" Romeo called out as he sat on his stoop for a moment and watched Maybelle scurry away, hoping she'd be okay walking home alone. As her bubbly bounce rounded the corner, he journeyed inside.

"Romeo! Romeo! Where have you been?"

Life Two

Dennis screamed as he opened the door at the sound of scratching from the other side. "You've never been out this long. And look at you, you're a mess!"

If you only knew, Romeo thought to himself.

Dennis scooped him up with both arms and carried him into the kitchen. Romeo's body hung like a rag, his back legs dangling. His tiny nose caught the smell of garlic meatballs and burnt cake. They were the leftover scents from Mrs. Crumb's Friday night card game. As always, Mr. Crumb was out with the guys, bar hopping alongside his faithful umbrella.

"What has gotten into you?" Dennis asked as he held Romeo high above his head, carefully inspecting his entire feline body. Romeo meowed and squirmed as Dennis continued his exam. He poked and pawed and tickled in all the right places as Mrs. Crumb walked in.

"Whatcha doing, Dennis?" she asked biting into a gooey sardine. "That cat looks like he's been taking a mud bath." She dragged her slippers along the tiled floor. "Why don't you be a good son and help me clean up the dishes?" Grabbing her apron from behind the cabinet door, she tied it tightly around her thick middle, slipped on her big, yellow, rubber gloves and handed Dennis a sponge. "You wash, I'll dry."

Dennis gave his mom a funny look and put Romeo down. He slicked back Romeo's ratty hair, which was tangled and wet and smelled like the city. Romeo liked it when Dennis petted him. It made him feel safe and loved. Tonight he needed that more than ever.

From the floor, Romeo watched Dennis help his mother scrape some sort of icky goop off the pots and pans in the kitchen sink with a spatula. When Mrs. Crumb walked by she gave Romeo a quick pat on the head, but unknowingly stepped on his paw. Romeo let out a meek, little yelp.

Later on, Romeo took a sluggish trip to the litter box and joined Dennis on the couch. Together they sat in the glow of the TV under an ugly blanket Grandma Crumb had knitted. It was bright pink with tiny, orange, crocheted flowers. By the end of the evening, Romeo had destroyed one of the flowers with his claws. Dennis did the same.

"Boy, Romeo," Dennis said. "You sure are quiet tonight."

Before going to bed, Romeo and Dennis listened cluelessly to the news. Mr. Crumb insisted that his son watch it every night, and Dennis insisted his cat join him. Mr. Crumb stressed the importance of learning about the world, not just the city.

On the fuzzy screen the pretty, young newscaster talked about boring things like labor unions, pickets, and walkouts. The only segment the two buddies did enjoy was the weather report. At least they could understand it. Dennis liked to know how much more rain there would be. It had a huge effect on his baseball league. He loved baseball and played third base. So

Life Two

far, they had only practiced twice the whole season. And one of those times Dennis was forced to go home for throwing a mud ball at Jeffrey Newberg's butt. At any rate, Romeo and Dennis listened carefully as they watched the weather map.

"Well, it has arrived folks. El Queso is here!" smiled the funny looking weatherman. He was short and stubby with thick, black-rimmed glasses and wore a green and blue plaid jacket with an ugly, wide tie. "It was hard not to notice the rain today. Remember, this is only the beginning, so stay dry if you can."

Dennis threw a pillow at the TV and shut it off with his big toe. He dusted cookie pieces off his lap and stretched high up toward the water-stained ceiling.

"Come on, Romeo," he said with a yawn. "Let's go to bed." Dennis and Romeo walked down the short, creaky hallway to Dennis' room.

"Dennis, did you brush your teeth?" Mrs. Crumb called from the bathtub.

"Yes, ma."

Romeo heard a splash. "*All* of your teeth?"

Dennis stopped near the bathroom and stared at the glow from under the door. "Yes! I brushed *all* my teeth right after dinner. Good night, mom."

"Good night, dear."

Inside his room, Dennis found a used toothpick. He grabbed it from the garbage and began to chisel away at the bits of meatballs stuck between

Chapter Two

his teeth. He ran his tongue over the plaque build-up then tossed the pick back in the wastebasket. "Good enough," he mumbled.

Romeo sat near the doorway and watched Dennis get ready for bed as he did every night. He tossed his muddy sneakers and faded jeans on the floor and put on his old pajama bottoms. They nearly came up to his knees like shorts. Then Dennis threw his mismatched socks at Romeo. The sweaty stench was far too much, even for a cat to bear. Romeo ventured over to the window for some air.

"Come here, Romeo," Dennis called, snuggling under his cozy covers. Romeo ignored him. He knew Dennis would be sound asleep in a matter of seconds. Romeo usually slept on the corner of Dennis' pillow. If he got hungry during the night, he liked to chew at the edges of the cowboy pillowcase. It wasn't as good as a freshly killed mouse, but it passed the time.

Romeo looked up at Dennis' desk that sat directly in front of the window. It was sprinkled with old, worn toys, frayed magazines, and comic books. A thick layer of dust had formed on the chair, and a dead potted plant sat in an open drawer on a mildewed water stain. Behind the plant was a crumpled up girly picture Dennis bought at school from Manny Fillmore. He paid five cents and two pieces of gum for it. The girl in the picture wore next to nothing. Dennis looked at it only once, and shoved it into his desk when he heard his father's footsteps. It had been hiding there ever since.

Romeo's eyes went over to the far window. It was slightly open, allowing the cold breeze to blow and twist the sheer curtains. He swallowed a big gulp of courage and jumped up, planting himself on the sill to look out at the foggy city below. The rain was still coming down like the weatherman had said. Some unlucky folks were out there clinging to their hats and other belongings. Romeo couldn't see any cats, though he knew their sneaky little selves were out there in the shadows. Maybe even Fidel.

Romeo's nose followed the breeze that lifted his head straight at Gwen's bedroom window across the alley. It was open, along with the pretty, white drapes. Gwen usually kept them open, unless she thought Dennis or one of his pesky friends was trying to look in. One time she was slipping on a new purple dress for her birthday party when she glanced over and saw Dennis' nose peeking through the curtains. She told her mom, who told Mrs. Crumb. Dennis was sternly warned that if he ever spied on her again, he'd be forced to eat liver for a month. Lunch and dinner! Dennis hated liver, almost as much as he hated that dreadful purple dress.

On the left side of Gwen's room lay a mountain of old dolls. Their cracked, porcelain faces had creepy little smiles, and they wore handmade lacy dresses. He remembered seeing Gwen stuffing Queen Elizabeth into one of the more unflattering frocks. Her fluffy,

Chapter Two

Life Two

yellow fur stuck out between each ivory button. She was humiliated.

Beyond the dolls was Gwen herself. She lay there all alone in her pale blue nightgown. In her hand she clutched a cat toy. It was a ball with a bell inside, Queen Elizabeth's favorite. She loved to chase it all over the apartment. Sometimes late at night Romeo swore he heard the little bell ringing. As Gwen held the toy tightly, she cried and cried. Romeo's heart sank, and he cried too. Oh, how he would miss his friend.

"Come on, Romeo," Dennis nudged as he shut the curtains. "Let's go to bed."

Before jumping down Romeo reached one paw up to the window, felt the cold glass and whispered, "Goodbye, Queen Elizabeth."

Chapter Three

Sunday morning Romeo saw Gwen's father carrying out a small cardboard box. A casket for Queen Elizabeth? A death tomb? The tall man hurried down the stoop wearing a heavy raincoat and soggy, fur hat. His face was twisted and scrunched from the wind. Immediately he and the brown box slipped into a grimy cab and drove away.

By Monday morning Romeo had to get out. Sitting home alone was not helping his mood. Dennis' room was far too depressing. So, after Dennis left for school, Romeo slipped out of the window and climbed down to the street. He headed toward the Factory.

Romeo walked down the crowded sidewalk feeling anxious and nervous. Surely Fidel was out there somewhere. Romeo was almost at the Factory when he heard a startling noise. It sounded like a screaming

Life Two

cat. Immediately, he ducked behind an old man's leg, clinging onto his thrift store pants. His little heart pounded from fright.

"Get off'a me, ya dumb cat!" the old man howled shaking Romeo from his ankle. To Romeo he smelled like stale cheese.

The angry man shook his leg and tugged at his pants. Romeo finally let go after being kicked twice with a thick, rubber sole. The man stumbled away grumbling something nasty, jiggling his thick ankle as he went.

Just as he was about to dart across the street, Romeo heard the eerie shriek again. It was coming from behind a nearby hat shop. This time to his astonishment, he heard, "Romeo." He stopped in his tracks. Was this a joke? Who was out there calling to him?

Romeo slyly crept toward the voice, inching his way ever so cautiously. He heard his name called two more chilling times. As he reached the hat shop, he poked his nose around the corner.

"Oh my!" Romeo screamed. "Twinkle Toes! What are you doing here? You scared me to death!"

There, on the drippy ground was Twinkle Toes, all wrapped up in a newspaper, shivering and clutching tightly to the paper's edge. Because of the rain, the ink bled all over Twinkle's white patches of fur. He looked pathetic and miserable. The alleyway itself was like all the others, dark and creepy and full of discarded junk.

"Please, buddy," Twinkle Toes mumbled, lifting up his shaky head. "I'm s-s-s-so cold. I've been here all w-w-weekend." His bottom jaw shook furiously up and down. Romeo could hear Twinkle's stomach growling and noticed a large, obvious bump at the back of his head. Little chunks of dried blood poked out of its center.

Romeo stared at him in disbelief. "What the...? I don't understand."

Suddenly, a loud banging vibrated from the hat shop. It startled Romeo so, that he ducked under the soggy newspapers alongside his friend. Then, another series of noises erupted, riotous, yelling noises. The two cats quivered together under the headlines and not-so-funny funnies.

Then, like a bolt of lightening, the hat shop door exploded open, and a stout, scruffy man leapt out. He was wearing black rain boots and a long brown coat. His face looked mean, and his fists tough.

"That's it! I quit!" the man screamed from outside the shop. "And I'm never coming back to this dump ever again!" Just then, somebody inside whipped a hat in his direction, and the door slammed shut. The bitter man kicked the hat savagely out of his way and stomped down the street splashing mud all over his boots.

Romeo and Twinkle Toes peeked up from behind the newspaper as the man turned a corner and slipped out of sight. Romeo stood up and shook off some of the ink that had seeped into his fur. "Close call," he said, his teeth chattering. "Now, tell me what you're doing

Life Two

here. And why do you look so terrible?"

From under the soggy paper Twinkle Toes confessed, "*You* know why. It's *them*! They did it again."

"Fidel?" Romeo's heart began to race. "You mean Fidel did this?" He slunk down quickly and took a scattered look around.

"No man, it wasn't Fidel. It was *them*!" Twinkle whined.

"Oh, you mean...your people?" Only a few days earlier Twinkle Toes painfully blabbed of the three lives he'd lost at the cruel hands of his people. He was starved, beaten, and soaked. They had been forcing him to sleep on the porch no matter how hard it rained. He had been sick and tired and depressed for weeks.

"Yes," Twinkle Toes sobbed. "I don't know what to do, man."

Romeo cautiously glanced around the alley and concentrated. Being there so soon after the vicious attack made him nervous. Very nervous. "First thing we have to do is get out of here. We shouldn't be in an alley, no way." Romeo tossed the paper off Twinkle Toes and helped him to stand up. As he did, he spotted another bump at the back of Twinkle's left leg, and another near his right. Everywhere he looked Twinkle Toes was in bad shape.

Twinkle Toes wobbled as he stood. Weak from hunger and soaked from the rain, it was obvious to Romeo that he was in serious trouble and in need of

Chapter Three

immediate attention. Putting aside his own woes, Romeo focused on the matter at hand. He couldn't lose another friend. "Let's get you out of here and back to the Factory where it's safe, then we'll think of a plan. There's no way you're going back to those *people*," Romeo huffed.

Twinkle Toes looked at Romeo with his dazed, blurry eyes and said, "I hate to do this to you, Romeo, I mean, after what you've been through, but thanks buddy."

As they scurried from the alley, a pointy little head popped up from a garbage can filled with old, leather soles from the shoemaker's shop. It was Bait. He knew Fidel, his *demanding* boss, would be pleased to know what he had just witnessed. Fidel kept Bait around for his impeccable spying skills, lurking being his specialty. His ratty, mangled self had lurked him into many dangerous situations.

Bait wiggled his way up, spitting some leather from his mouth. The battered, metal can fell over with a clang as he jumped out spilling all the smelly trash onto the alley floor. He headed straight for a nearby secret hideaway beyond a small hole in the brick alley wall. Little did he know one of the discarded shoe soles was stuck to his butt. What he did know was that Fidel and his cronies were waiting for him in the hideaway behind the garbage dump, hoping he had some juicy gossip.

Life Two

From outside Bait could hear Fidel's explosive ranting and raving for who knows why. He was yelling and smashing rocks and pieces of bricks against the wall. It sounded like a regular bar brawl in there. Bait took in a heavy breath of alley fumes and ventured inside. As he did, he purposely smashed a fly that was sailing downstream on a soggy potato chip. Like a bad blister, that dead fly would be stuck somewhere between Bait's toes all day.

Bait ducked through the pipe, crouching low. Very low. The pipe was cramped and damp and rang with an annoying patter of the rainy drip. At the far end was a small, fiery light glowing from inside. It came from Fidel's new and favorite toy, an old baby food jar he made Max fill with about one hundred fireflies. Max had worked diligently on the new light all weekend. The bugs were stuffed inside, one on top of the other like sardines. Fidel wore the lit jar on his collar along with his trophy ID tags he had taken off of dead Sticks, which now included Queen Elizabeth's. Fidel had made this conquest his most favorite and put Queenie's tag in front of all the others. It bounced and clinked behind the blazing bug jar, blurring her engraved name through the foggy glass. Already a bug had climbed to the top of the jar, screaming through one of the holes Fidel punctured with his needle-like claw. She desperately pleaded and begged to get out, promising Fidel many great and wonderful things if he would only spare her life. After all her courageous

27

Chapter Three

efforts, Fidel flicked her back down with a nasty laugh. It was torture for those poor bugs.

Bait snuck in and suctioned himself against the back wall that was actually a swelled wooden beam. Fidel noticed him cowering in the corner. "Come in, Bait," he said sharply. "Stop hiding and get your pathetic self in here!" Fidel stepped away from his cronies. They had been glued to the farthest wall since the rocks started flying. Fidel took a dramatic leap forward. "So, tell me," Fidel said seriously, "what's new out there today? Surely something exciting is going on this, the weekend of our great triumph."

Bait made certain there was no more rock ammunition near Fidel's paws. When certain, he answered, "Well, I waited for that Romeo kid yesterday at the Factory, but he never showed up. I was ready to give it to him, just like you said, boss." Bait imitated punching Romeo with his left paw as he laughed maniacally.

"Yeah, so?" Fidel barked.

Gulp. "Well, uh...so, since Romeo didn't show up, I followed his dumb friend Tinkle, or somethin' stupid like that. Anyways, he gots these funny paws, I don't know, something funny about them. So, he starts walkin' in circles around the city. It was making me crazy. I was gettin' tired!"

"Then why did you follow him?" Fidel asked impatiently, teeth clenched together.

"I don't know. I was bored, I guess."

Life Two

Fidel rolled his eyes as Bait continued. "Okay, so I was followin' this cat around, who by the way, looked lousy, if you ask me. He had more bumps than me, if you can imagine that." Bait reached up and tapped his paw on the three new bumps popping out of his head in a perfect triangle. One was from a person he bit, another from a newspaper stand he walked into near Smelly's Bar, and the last was from Fidel himself. That one hurt the most. "So, this cat walks into this very alley. Can you believe it? Well, I've never heard a cat moan da way he did. It was pathetic, like a little baby. He laid there till today, all wet and yucky. Cool, huh? I hid in the garbage can and..."

Just then, Fidel angrily interrupted him with smoke spouting from his ears. "You mean to tell me that you and a *Stick* were in this very alley and you didn't come and?...No, no, no!" he growled with phony composure. "Go on, *Bait*, tell me what happened next." He smiled an evil grin and hissed like a snake.

"Okay," Bait whispered with hesitation. "As I was sayin', he just sits there like an idiot for nearly two days. I watched him very carefully from the garbage can. Yep, Fidel, I think you would be very impressed with my spynessness." Bait lifted his proud nose high in the air even when he made up words. "And then, get this, your buddy *Romeo* comes walkin' up."

Fidel's eyes shot open. "Romeo? Did you say *Romeo*?"

"Yeah, Romeo, in the flesh. I mean, he was

breathin' and everythin'. But, then he talks to the Tinkle guy, and helps him up, and takes him away somewheres. What do ya think?" Bait started to pick his teeth with the smidge of skin at the end of his tail, waiting for Fidel to speak.

Fidel took a long, disgusted look at Bait. He walked in two slow, complete circles around him, and like a slow building earthquake, Fidel started to rumble. It grew from there, his insides bubbling fiercer and fiercer. His eyes bugged out and his chest filled with air. "What do I think? What do I think? I think you are the most pathetic cat in the city! You just sat there? Watching a Stick? And not just *any* Stick! For two whole days you watched from a pile of garbage when I was only thirty paws away? And you don't come and tell me about it until Romeo and the other Stick are *gone*? Bait, you're going to get it for this one!" Fidel hissed, fire in his eyes.

Bait, feeling the size of a peanut, crouched to the floor, tail stuck tightly between his legs. Fidel lunged with a devilish growl, landing on Bait like a falling piano. The cronies in the back turned the other way as soon as the *punishment* began. They could hear Bait's garbled wails and cries. He was getting it, and he was getting it good. When Fidel finally stepped away, Bait lay in a pile of his own fur and drool. Bumps four and five were added to his growing collection.

Fidel's pulse still raced as he paced and mumbled uncontrollably. His body began to sweat, and his teeth gnashed back and forth. The fireflies in his baby jar necklace were jolted up and down, knocking off some legs and a few heads.

"I don't get it boss," Bait meekly said from under his fur pile. "What's the big deal?"

Fidel turned sharply and slithered over to him. He pressed his paw hard against bumps four and five and said in a controlled growl. "Obviously, you fool, if Romeo can just casually walk into an alley and have a conversation with his dear little friend, then we have accomplished nothing! Nothing! He doesn't fear us! He thinks he runs the city!"

Fidel released his paw from Bait's bumps. Bait moaned loudly, allowing the blood to rush back into his head.

"I told that little nuisance that I had a job to finish, and that's just what I'm going to do!" Fidel blasted.

"Really, boss, you mean it?" Bait asked, a safe distance away.

Fidel twirled his whiskers. "Of course, I'm serious! I've got to come up with something good, not just for that blasted Romeo but for all those loser Sticks. Once and for all they'll learn who's the boss in this city!" He turned to his pack. "Boys, be prepared to work. I have a feeling you are going to be very busy...*very* busy." With that, Fidel began to laugh uncontrollably, piercing everyone's eardrums. Soon, the entire place shook from the ruckus that spewed from the stench of Fidel's mouth, a torture unto itself.

Chapter Four

At the Factory Romeo led Twinkle Toes up to the medicine room. There, he received special attention, and even a mouse to eat. His visit caused something of a commotion, but not as much as the fact that Romeo had returned. Everybody wanted to talk to him, though nobody wanted to be the first. Romeo sat alone in the library thumbing through a geography book, looking at the colorful maps until some of his friends entered the room.

"Uh...hey, Romeo," Fluffy said, dressed in frilly blue socks. "Looks like Twinkle Toes is going to be just fine."

Romeo nodded his head, keeping his eyes in the book.

"Yeah, isn't that great?" Tabitha nudged enthusiastically. "Thanks to you, that is." She paused a moment and continued. "Say, Romeo, we're all sorry about what happened the other day, I mean-."

"Yeah, buddy. We's real sorry," Snickers cut in.

Romeo felt a knot well up in this throat. His eyes got glossy and filled with tears. He looked more heartbroken than any puppy dog ever had. "Thanks, guys," he said at last. "Thanks for everything."

"Hey, Romeo," Tabitha said. "Your voice is back to normal. No more stutter! Mr. Sox was right."

Romeo smiled and went back to his maps.

"All right, then," Fluffy added, "I guess we'll be seein' you."

All three cats turned and slowly headed for the soup pot. No one made a peep aside from the grumbling in Snicker's empty belly. Suddenly they heard something from behind. "Wait, guys. Come back!" It was Romeo, and he was ready to talk.

They all sat together on a large, dusty, crimson pillow, one on each corner, a golden tassel by their side. All eyes were on Romeo.

"Do you want to know what it was like?" Romeo asked slowly.

"What what's like?" Snickers answered, chewing on the golden fringe.

Fluffy punched him with his paw sending him tumbling off the pillow. "Death, you idiot! Do we want to know what death's like?"

"Oh, that," Snickers said dumbfounded, rubbing his sore shoulder.

Chapter Four

Tabitha's eyes grew wide. "Yes, Romeo! Tell us! Tell us what it's like. Did it hurt? Could you feel your insides squirming and your heart stopping?" She twisted and tugged at the pillow in anticipation.

"Well," Romeo began, "it really all happened so fast. I felt like I was falling down a long pipe. It was dark and musty in there, and I could hardly see a thing. Then I saw weird, smoky shadows that looked like different cats, mean ones, ugly ones, all waving me over... somewhere. I went toward them, but kind of in slow motion. It was scary. They were all laughing and cackling, like Alleys do." Romeo shuddered. He licked his lips. "Then, the tunnel, or whatever it was, started to spin. The faster it whirled me around, the more my head pounded and pounded. I was twirling so fast, I couldn't even see my own body. It was a total blur. In fact, everything looked hazy and spooky."

They stared in amazement.

"Well, it was kind of like that, all murky and blurry, just like puddles. And my head hurt really bad, worse than any headache ever. I think it was from the rock I fell on, because that hurt more than anything. I sure don't want to fall on a rock like that ever again!"

"Yikes!" Snickers sympathized.

"Anyway, I could feel myself coming to the end of this place. It was then that I heard all you guys calling my name, but I felt as if I couldn't move. I tried and tried, but it was just impossible, like I had fallen into some cement. Then, it got bright and I saw...I saw..." His eyes drifted away almost in a hypnotized stare.

"Go on, Romeo," Tabitha insisted. "Please!"

"Awe, nothing, I guess I just blacked out at that point. I don't really remember anything else."

Just then, the classroom door opened from the opposite end of the library. In came Mr. Sox along with three brand new little kittens, all younger than Romeo. Snickers and Tabitha went running toward them, but Fluffy stayed with Romeo.

"Hey, Romeo," Fluffy hesitated.

"Yeah, Fluff."

"What were you going to say back there? Why so secretive?"

"What are you talking about?" Romeo asked, shifty-eyed.

Fluffy gave him a stare and nudged him in the back. "Come on, buddy, I'm your best friend. Tell me. What did you see? You know, when you were dead?"

Romeo looked over at Mr. Sox and the new cats. "Like I said, I guess that's when I blacked out. The next thing I remember was waking up here, in the Factory. Honest."

"I don't know, Romeo. I don't believe you, not this time." He nudged Romeo again and tussled his fur. The two friends laughed and smiled together for the first time in days. It felt good. They rolled around on the pillows until Mr. Sox walked over. By then, they were giggling underneath the thick stuffing, their two little tails sticking straight out at either end.

Chapter Four

"Romeo?" Mr. Sox called from behind. He cleared his throat to sound more important. "Romeo!"

Romeo wiggled a bit and faced Mr. Sox. He saw the three little kittens looking up at him with big, innocent, blue eyes like sweet pieces of candy. He wanted to tell them all to run home and never come out again. The city was too dangerous for tiny kittens, too vile for Sticks. While Romeo stood there, they fidgeted and played with loose threads in the rug, feisty and rambunctious without a care in the world.

"I'm glad you came back, Romeo," Mr. Sox said joyfully. "I was worried. But I said to myself, Romeo's a smart male, he'll come back to us."

Romeo looked at him and grinned. "Yes, Mr. Sox, I couldn't stay away too long, even though this place brings back sad memories for me, you know, with *her* not here."

Mr. Sox walked closer to Romeo and placed his old paw against his. "I know, son," he comforted. "We all miss her. But life must go on, and that's just what's happening here. In fact, I'd like you to meet a brand new group of Sticks."

Snickers and the others gathered around as Mr. Sox stood near the first kitten on the left. A female. She was abnormally fat for such a young thing, but had the prettiest blend of browns throughout her fur. "This is Tuesday," he introduced. "She comes to us from the 51st block. Waldo spotted her in a window chewing on a piece of steak fat looking bored, so he called her down."

Life Two

"Hi, Tuesday!" Snickers said enthusiastically.

Tuesday glanced up from the frayed rug and gave Snickers a snotty smirk and a long, unfriendly blink. She rolled her eyes and went back to her string pulling. Snickers' grin faded to a look of hurt.

"And this fine fellow is Delio," Mr. Sox continued, pulling a tiny, black and white kitten closer. "He lives near Calvin."

Romeo looked Delio up and down. He had a funny, round face with the smallest black nose. His whiskers were curly, and his ears faced backwards. Perhaps the oddest thing about his appearance was the slight hint of a black beard beneath his chin.

"I live with two fishes, two snakes, one bird, and one Cocker Spaniel," Delio squeaked, his nose high in the air.

"A Cocker Spaniel? What's a Cocker Spaniel?" Tabitha asked.

Mr. Sox interrupted, "A Spaniel, my dear, is a dog."

"A dog! You live with a real live dog?" Snickers yelled. "Does he smell?"

"Sometimes," Delio snarled. "I tell him what to do, and he listens." Delio's mind drifted off to the time he held the Spaniel down with his claw and savagely plucked out three hairs from his head. He grinned.

"That's not true. There's no way you can tell a dog what to do," Fluffy remarked. "What do you think about this, Mr. Sox? I mean, a cat living with a dog? No way!"

Chapter Four

Mr. Sox walked in a tight circle around the cats. He twitched his whiskers and squinted his eyes. He sat down at his favorite old chair and remarked, "Yes, yes, I have heard of these things before. Cats living with dogs. It's foreign to most of us, but it does happen. I, personally, have never met a cat that lived with a dog until this very day, though I have heard stories, strange stories of such a happening. But I will say this, I hardly believe that you are in charge of a dog, Delio, even if it is a Cocker Spaniel."

Everyone looked at Delio. He whined, "It's true! It's true! I tell him what to...." Just then, Delio's eyes caught the shadow of a passing cat on the far wall. Instinctively, he lunged at it with all his might smashing into the cracked wood. He fell to the floor with a thud. Embarrassed, he sat there alone.

Hiding behind Mr. Sox was the third kitten. He was red and orange with droopy, scared eyes. His stubby, little legs shook and wobbled. "Now, where's Murphy?" Mr. Sox called out. He reached behind him and felt Murphy's coarse coat. "Ah, yes, there you are. Come on out, nobody's going to hurt you. Come along now."

Little by little, Murphy inched his way from under a chair. He kept his eyes at paw level. Dangling from his mouth was a string he proudly captured from the rug.

"Hi, Murphy," Romeo finally said. "My name's Romeo, and these are my friends Fluffy, Tabitha, and

Life Two

Snickers. We're all about six months old." Everyone smiled at Murphy. "How old are you?"

"Don't know," he said meekly, returning to his spot under the chair. He stared oddly at Fluffy's blue sock.

Mr. Sox reached down and patted his head. "Don't worry about a thing, Murphy. You're going to be just fine. I know all this can take some getting used to."

Murphy looked up at him with adoring eyes. Romeo remembered how scary it was being the new guy. Queen Elizabeth had made it so easy for him. He hoped to do the same for these little ones.

Just then, the soup pot rose from the first floor. Vittles and Mr. Shadow got out. They looked excited and anxious. With heavy, long steps, they approached Mr. Sox.

"Sir," Mr. Shadow began, "I think we are ready now for the..." Suddenly, Mr. Shadow slipped on his own tail and fell, barreling into a stack of dusty books.

Vittles chuckled and continued. "As he was *about* to say, we are ready for you downstairs, Mr. Sox."

"Um, I've got to go now, children," Mr. Sox said secretively. "I'll catch up with you later." He put on his foggy glasses and walked off with Vittles and Mr. Shadow.

Fluffy quickly caught up with them. "Can I go too, Mr. Sox? Can I? Can I?" He bounced around in circles like a kangaroo.

Chapter Four

"No, Fluffy, not this time," Mr. Shadow said in a deep voice. "We've got...work to do." He pulled his yellow, knit sleeves down to his paws and continued on. Ahead, Vittles was already waiting in the soup pot.

"But, we never get to go with you guys," Fluffy yelled back. "I'm not a little kitten anymore, in case you haven't noticed!"

Mr. Sox and Mr. Shadow both gave Fluffy a harsh stare. "Goodbye, for now," Mr. Sox concluded. "Why don't you show the new kittens around the building? By then we'll be finished with our meeting."

Romeo, Fluffy, and Tabitha stared at the new Sticks that were chewing on their paws and chasing their tails. Romeo and his friends let out a breath of disappointment, though Snickers delighted in the tuna scraps he found in his fur. As the kittens romped, they jealously watched the three older cats disappear out of sight to their place of mystery.

Chapter Five

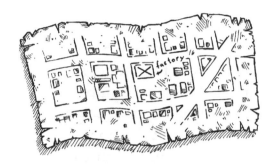

Mr. Sox, Mr. Shadow, and Vittles went in to a secret, private room on the first floor. It was located deep in the back of Waldo's photography lab beyond a tiny blue door, hidden behind an old file cabinet. The metal drawers were filled with the personal records of long ago umbrella employees. Though Mr. Sox disapproved, now and then Waldo sifted through the files reading about the dark and scandalous secrets of the umbrella staff. There was Cindy, the bookkeeper, caught stealing money to finance her long, lonely nights wallowing away at the local bar, or Clown-face Charlie, the German umbrella handle designer, who was so ugly he legally had to keep his face covered at all times. And, of course, the Durango sisters who were Siamese twins joined at the butt. Perhaps Waldo's most favorite file to scour through belonged to Lou, the man who insisted on wearing his ex-girlfriend's prom dress to work everyday. A lovely lime green chiffon, or so the story goes.

Despite the temptations, Waldo was given first dibs on Roy and Yellowtail's fish selection as incentive to keep the files and the room's whereabouts hush-hush. In its day, the room was probably used as a storage space. When Lulu first started the Factory, it was filled with boxes and boxes of umbrella handles, which had since been thrown away in a dump by the Sticks. Now, the small room was used by Mr. Sox and other elder Sticks for restricted, secret meetings.

The three cats crept in through the tiny, blue door. It creaked loudly. The room itself felt cold and forgotten. The last time they were there was over a year ago when they secretly discussed a dead Stick found beaten in a mailbox. On the dirty floor lay a large piece of white paper with lines and words written all over it held down by a large rock at each corner. Vittles had put it there earlier that day. Mr. Sox lowered his glasses and carefully inspected the paper. He nodded and mumbled to himself, making funny faces as he thought. Vittles watched nervously. "So you see, Mr. Sox," Vittles began, "this is what I propose for all Sticks. Combat classes are the only way to protect us from Fidel. No offense but the City Safety course Mr. Shadow teaches isn't enough to fight off the Alleys. We need heavy duty, military-style battle classes to prepare us for any eventuality, no matter how violent it gets. We can't afford another tragedy like last week." He dropped his head at the sad memory. "What do you think, Mr. Sox?"

Mr. Sox walked in a full circle around the plan that lay in front of him. On it was a class schedule, a detailed map of the Factory and the city, and drawings of cats in fighting poses. "Combat class, eh? Humph. What is this city coming to?" He shook his head with sorrow. "Tell me, Vittles, how do you suppose we orchestrate these classes?"

"Well, I say we work in groups of about thirty. That is, thirty Sticks per class. There will be three classes taught by me, Mr. Shadow, and Waffles, and they will meet everyday. Attendance is *absolutely* mandatory! And yes, they'll be grueling and tough! The Sticks won't be happy. But, we *have* to do this for our own protection. If and when Fidel attacks again, we must be ready to *crush* him! Grind his body into yucky pieces!" Vittles slapped his fist to the floor.

"Yes, and those classes will be?" Mr. Sox asked as he sat down.

Mr. Shadow stepped forward like a soldier. "One class will be a much more intense version of my City Safety class only we'll delve deeper into the ins and outs of the city, focusing on the outs, such as secret passageways. Vittles will set up the War Strategy Workshops, approved by you, of course, in the event of an attack. They will consist of battle plans, how to think under pressure, and intense strategizing. Remember, at this point we do not plan on staging any attacks of our own. We are primarily interested in defense. However, the best defense is a good offense. We will make the Alleys afraid to attack us because we will be prepared."

"He's right!" Waffles jumped in. "And finally, all Sticks will join me everyday for the Workout Training." He punched his two front paws together and flexed his big muscles. "I think this will be the most important part of their day. All males and females will be put through a rigorous workout. You know, to get them in tip-top shape. In addition to the exercise, I will be teaching them defensive moves. Everyone needs to know how to fight off a pack of angry Alleys. Just think, if we had this training last week, perhaps Queen Elizabeth would still be alive."

Mr. Sox stroked the gray fur atop his head. He pushed his glasses higher up his nose and brushed some dust from his tail. His regal face looked sad and broken. He was getting too old to be worrying about such things. His hopes for a peaceful future had once again been slapped by the sting of reality. Combat classes? Mandatory workouts? War strategy? These were times he hoped he'd never see. "All right," he sighed. "We have to get started right away. Vittles, you announce the program. Be tough. Let them know there will be consequences for *any* absences. No excuses. Shadow, make a copy of the schedule and hang it in the rec room where everyone can see. And have Waffles set up a guard duty schedule. If you males are teaching classes, we will need substitute guards. I think you'll agree that additional guard posts around the Factory should be implemented as well. Now, if you will excuse me, I'm going home." Without a goodbye, Mr. Sox crawled back through the tiny blue door and left the Factory. He would spend the rest of the day sleeping as distressing, stressful dreams rumbled in his head.

Mr. Shadow gathered up the paper from the floor and tried to stuff it into his brown, leather bag, though terribly unsuccessful. He tangled himself in the bag's strap and accidentally slapped himself with the paper, somehow managing to twist his sweater over his head. He ripped the entire left side of the paper and got four paper cuts on his paw in the process.

"Oh, just gimme that!" Vittles finally yelled, pulling the paper out from under him. "I can't watch this another second." He grabbed the crumpled mess and folded it neatly until it formed a perfect square. "There."

Later that day, Romeo and Twinkle Toes ate lunch together. Roy and Yellowtail only had three shrimp tails and one smelly fish head left, all the good stuff was eaten by Snickers and Waldo. With his paw, Romeo gouged out the fish eyes and flung them at Twinkle Toes.

"Ha! Ha!" Romeo laughed. "Gotcha!"

"Hey, quit it!" Twinkle Toes hollered, scraping gooey fish eyes from his cheek. "Dude, why are you in such a good mood all of the sudden?"

Chapter Five

Romeo looked at him innocently. "I'm not. I'm just trying not to think about everything...that's all."

Twinkle nuzzled up to Romeo and smiled. "In that case, you can throw fish eyes at me any time," he laughed.

Later that day, Mr. Shadow, Waffles, and Vittles were hard at work planning and scheduling the combat classes. With a little luck, they would be ready to make the announcement to the Sticks the very next day. When it was time to go home, Romeo caught sight of Twinkle Toes dragging his sad, little body out the door.

"Hey, Twinkles!" Romeo called. "Wait up!"

Twinkle Toes stopped but didn't turn around. "Later, Romeo. I'll see you tomorrow."

"No, Twink, you can't go home, not after...They'll kill you! Besides, look at you. You're a mess."

Twinkle Toes looked down at his ratty fur, which had once been shiny and smooth. He cringed at the thought of going back home to those monsters he lived with, but what else was a Stick to do? Surely they would be extra mad at him for being out all weekend. Still, Twinkle Toes knew he needed to go. Maybe, just maybe, they would be nice like they used to be. "I gotta go, dude," he waved as he headed for the door.

Romeo struggled for something to say as he watched his friend walk farther and farther away. Instantly, a thought crossed his mind. "Wait! I've got an idea, and it just might work!" Romeo shouted as he dashed after his forlorn friend.

Life Two

"Look man, I already told you, I gotta get--."

Suddenly, Romeo bit Twinkle Toes hard in the tail with his sharp, tiny teeth and mumbled, "Shut up! Get me a piece of paper and a pencil."

"Youch!" Twinkle Toes screamed. "You're serious!" He did as Romeo asked, and within a minute he returned with a crumpled piece of torn paper and a chewed up number two pencil.

Immediately, Romeo grabbed the pencil from Twinkle Toes' teeth and began to tap his own nose. He stared blankly at the ceiling, making funny puckering noises with his lips. "Hmmm," he mused to himself. "What should I write?"

Twinkle Toes was getting restless and worried at the thought of arriving home much later. He wasn't in the mood for a beating. "Will you tell me what's going on already, weirdo?"

"Got it," Romeo snapped, a proud grin painting his face. "Genius!"

Romeo flattened out the paper on one of the rec room's wooden tables. He wiggled into a chair and stood up on his hind legs. With his right paw he frantically scribbled down some words. He stopped for a moment, chewed on the pink eraser then added one last word. "There," he said pleased. "That oughta do it." With the paper in his mouth, Romeo jumped off the chair and gave it to Twinkle Toes. "Read it," he muttered.

Twinkle Toes pulled it closer and cleared his

throat. He looked around the room making sure no one else was watching. When ready, he began.

Dearest Gwen,

You lost a good friend, but I could be one too.

Please take me home,

Twinkle Toes

He put the paper down and yelled, "What? You crazy, Romeo? Go and live with Gwen? Jeez, bro, you've really lost it." He began to walk away.

"No!" Romeo called. "Come on, Toes. Do you really want to go back to those awful people? Is that what Queen Elizabeth would have wanted you to do? Use your head!"

Twinkle Toes stopped.

"Look, you've got a chance," Romeo pleaded. "I don't know if she'll take you, but you've got to give it a try, don't you?"

Twinkle Toes twisted his bumpy head and looked directly at Romeo. His mouth turned down, and he nodded.

Life Two

Soon after, the two males were heading down 13th Street toward Gwen's home, the note tucked under Twinkle's collar. With a sharp rock, Romeo scratched off his real address and phone number from his ID tag. The plan was simple. Toes would wait outside for Gwen to come home from school, which would be soon. When he spotted her, he would nuzzle up to her ankles and meow. If all went well, the rest would be history. Unfortunately, the note was getting all wet. A fierce storm dropped sheets of rain from the sky. They splashed loudly against the cement and shook the city. Twinkle Toes was getting more nervous. "This isn't going to work, dude," he said disappointed as a huge drop of rain crashed on his face. "The note's not going to make it!"

Romeo darted and zigzagged from awning to awning, leading Twinkle Toes in his path. "Sure it will work. Just protect that note!"

After another wave of rainwater, Twinkle Toes stopped. He sat under a barber's sign huffing and puffing gasps of air into his lungs. Romeo was way ahead. As he ran, he took a quick look back. "What are you doing, Twinkle Toes? Come on!"

"Forget it, Romeo! I'm tired. Besides, the note is all soggy."

"So what. She'll still be able to read it. Gwen's a smart girl. Get up now! I mean it!"

Weak and worn out, Twinkle Toes forced himself back into stride. By now the note was all wet and starting to rip. "There," Romeo pointed, eying a dry spot. "You should wait over there. I'll watch from the window until you're safe."

"Wait a minute," Twinkle Toes interrupted. "You're not going to stay with me, pal? This was your idea in the first place."

"Yeah, but I thought you could just--."

Suddenly, Romeo's little body was scooped up into a familiar hand. It belonged to Dennis who had returned from school, and he wasn't alone.

"Ah ha! Caught ya!" Dennis laughed, lifting Romeo high up into the air.

"Hey, put him down, Dennis. You'll hurt him," whined Joey Magpee from behind his yellow, plastic rain hat. Joey was in Dennis' fifth grade class. Now and then Joey's mom made them play together. Joey had no other friends, and Dennis didn't mind as long as nobody from school found out. Joey had six fingers on each hand and teeth the size of wafers.

"Naw, he won't get hurt. This is my guy, Romeo. I could throw him up to the window, and he wouldn't even get a scratch. Wanna see?" Dennis held Romeo like a football.

"Meow!!!" Romeo cried.

"Aw, I'm just kidding. Come on, let's go inside and get some corned beef nuggets." Dennis flung Romeo over his shoulder and searched his pockets for his key. He found it in the back left one underneath some chewed gum he hid from his teacher. As Dennis and Joey headed to the front entrance, Romeo looked in Twinkle Toes' direction. He was sitting in the dry spot Romeo had found for him with a most pathetic look on his face. While Dennis bobbed Romeo up and down over his shoulder, Romeo motioned to Twinkle with his paw to stay there and wait. Soon, Romeo, Dennis, and Joey disappeared into the big building leaving Twinkle Toes all alone.

Nearly twenty minutes passed, and Twinkle Toes began to get worried. He wondered if perhaps Gwen went to a friend's house, or maybe to one of those doll shops that little girls frequented. The more he thought about it, the more restless he became. At this late hour, if he were to go to his home, he would most definitely spend the night on the porch. Another soggy, cold night would surely kill him…again. To make matters worse, Twinkle Toes knew that somewhere upstairs Romeo was watching down from his warm windowsill, probably munching a tasty morsel.

Twinkle Toes stretched his neck far enough to see down the long block. There was no sign of Gwen. Actually, he didn't even know who she was. Romeo only told him that she was a cute girl with blond curly hair who wore an oversized blue raincoat with flowers stenciled on the collar.

After several people rushed by, he finally caught sight of a blond girl in a blue coat. *That must be her*, he thought to himself. *I'm saved*. Instantly, Twinkle Toes felt a tinge of relief shiver through his entire body. He stepped toward the sidewalk and prepared himself for a sure-fire, irresistible, sweetie pie nuzzle. Unsuspecting Gwen was certain to snatch him up because he was so cute and innocent looking. Twinkle watched as the little girl walked closer. He couldn't see her face, though he knew it was somewhere under that floppy hood. Suddenly, a noise startled him from behind. It was a howling sound. Twinkle Toes swung his head around causing the note to jab him in the neck. When he looked up, he faced a most horrible sight. There were two grisly Alleys staring him right in the eyes. He didn't recognize them, though they were Alleys just the same, one male and one female, dripping wet and twice his size. Twinkle Toes began to back away quickly, but slipped in a puddle.

"Ha-ha!" one of the Alleys laughed sarcastically.

"What do we have here?" the other snapped.

They sandwiched Twinkle Toes tightly between their heavy bodies and hissed in his ears.

"Hey, Fink?" the first one said.

"Yeah, Honey?" the other replied, knocking Twinkle Toes in the shoulder.

Fink looked down. "Get a load of his feet! It's like he's got shoes on or somethin'."

"What a loser!" Honey added. "Don't you know anything, loser? Any cat who's got white feet is an automatic loser!"

Twinkle Toes was about to cry. "Come on, dudes,

let me go, whadaya say?"

"Hey," Fink said inching closer. He pointed with his left paw then grumbled, "What's wit the paper, fancy-feet?"

"It's nothing. Well, gotta go!"

Honey laughed and grabbed the paper from Twinkle's collar. She and Fink tossed it back and forth over Toes' quivering head. He pleaded with them to give it back. "You want this, loser?" Honey teased mercilessly, dangling the note in front of him. Then she slowly put it in her mouth and chewed.

"No!!!" Twinkle Toes yelled.

Fink laughed as Honey spit the chewed paper into the curb. It landed in a steady stream of rainwater. Twinkle ran from his captives and scrambled to get it as it floated for the gutter drifting closer and closer toward the sewer. Twinkle finally caught up to the soaked paper and stretched out his paw as far as he could to grab it. He missed. Standing there in the deep water, he watched his only prayer drift from sight. Enraged, he slowly turned and lunged for the Alleys. They darted away, laughing and mocking like the two bullies they were. "Loser feet!" they yelled. Twinkle Toes watched them disappear around a corner with thick foam bellowing from the corners of his mouth. It was all over. At a loss, he began to walk home, his head held low as he wept.

Toes had only taken a few steps when he heard another voice. "And who are you, little guy?" Twinkle

Chapter Five

Toes was ready to fight off the Alleys this time, his jagged claws extended. But when he looked up, he didn't find an Alley at all. He found a little girl with blond, curly hair and a long, blue raincoat with flowers stenciled on the collar. "Gosh," she said. "You must be freezing. Are you lost? You better come home with me."

Gwen scooped Twinkle Toes up and carried him inside. He finally felt calm. It was a feeling he had never experienced before, and he liked it.

"Thank you, Romeo," he said to himself.

Chapter Six

Back at Smelly's Bar, Fidel was busy gulping down his third thimble of beer. It tasted bitter and rancid, and slid down his throat like syrup. Sitting to his left was Bait, picking at a crusty scab, to his right, Stella. Stella was a bossy female cat with spiky, red fur and deep, yellow eyes. Her nails were long, sharp, and curled at the tips. Fidel was drawn to her.

They sat on two upside-down flowerpots at the center of the bar, their bodies devoured by specks of red light shining from above. Thumbs blew into his rusty saxophone at the back of the room, while Smelly cleaned out mugs with a dirty snot-rag at the bar.

"Hey, Smelly," Stella shouted rudely. "Pour me another beer, would ya?" She banged the empty thimble repeatedly against the bar. Unfortunately for Stella, Smelly had become mesmerized by a tasty worm.

Chapter Six

"I said, gimme another brewski!" she yelled again. "What's a gal gotta do to get a beer around dis joint?"

"I think the *lady* would like a beer," Fidel snapped. "If it's not too much *trouble*, Smelly."

Smelly scrambled over to the tub of beer and whimpered, "Oh, no, Fidel, one beer, coming right up for the lady." He frantically poured Stella her drink and casually glanced back for the worm. Sadly, it was gone.

"Thanks, doll," Stella charmed in a husky voice.

Fidel leaned in closer to give her a playful kiss, when he heard a sudden clamor at the door. There, in the jagged entrance stood a cat among the dark shadows. Fidel recognized the curvy shape. It belonged to Raven, his ex. "Delly? Where've you been?" she screeched. "Delly, what are you doin' with her?"

Fidel just ignored her.

Raven staggered closer to the bar. "Who is she, Delly? Huh? Who is this...tramp?"

Stella leaned back and gave Raven a nasty stare. Without opening her mouth, she sent her a long, low hiss. Bait chewed his tail so hard to keep himself from laughing, it started to drip Alley blood onto the floor.

"*Beat it*, Raven," Fidel said with a growl into his beer.

"But Delly?" Raven cried. "I...I don't understand!" Tears began to stream down her wet fur, and her legs started to wobble. She slung herself on the bar.

"Look, honey. The guy said *beat it*!" Stella yelled, shoving Raven away.

Life Two

Raven looked shocked. "Are you going to let her treat me like *that*, Delly?" she snapped.

Fidel finally faced Raven. Her eyes were bloodshot and her fur sloppy. Her claws weren't painted, nor were her fat lips. To him, she looked pathetic. And if there was one thing he hated, it was a pathetic groveler. He rolled his eyes and cracked, "Listen toots, Stella's my new thing, at least for now that is." Fidel and Stella nuzzled together and laughed sinisterly.

"I don't get it, Delly!" Raven pestered. "I mean, what about me? This is *our* place, you remember?"

"Quit the sweet talk, *sugar*, and get out!" Fidel exploded. Raven dashed toward the door in a frantic mess as everyone watched. Fidel threw a thimble at her, adding, "And stop calling me Delly!"

Bait chuckled, his tail blood soaked.

"Shut up, Bait!" Fidel roared, stomping on his tail to add insult to injury.

"Ouch!" Bait wailed.

"All right, back to business," Fidel said gulping his brew. "Now, listen everybody. We have to work hard, and we have to work fast. No slackers! Understood?"

His crew nodded their heads.

Fidel continued, "Now, Clank, Fink, and Mustard, did you find any carpet squares yet? You *better* tell me you did." He intimidatingly cracked all his paw knuckles against the bar.

Clank, Fink, and Mustard, all members of Fidel's lot, shook nervously from their table. They stared blankly at the walls, each waiting for the other to speak. Finally, seeing Fidel beginning to boil, Bait said, "Uh, yeah, Delly...I mean, Fidel, we's found a lot of them welcome mats and tings on porches and stuff."

"Oh?" Fidel asked bitingly. "And where might those pieces be?"

"They, uh, well, we haven't actually got 'em yet, see. We're gonna find all the good ones first, and then go get 'em in one swoop, just like the boxes you asked for. Yeah, uh...that's it, boss." He swallowed a deep, painful gulp.

"That better be it!" Fidel said sharply. "Because if it's not, there will be *hell* to pay! Three days! That's what you've got! Three days. And if it's not all here... crunch!" He tightened his paw into a crushing fist and grabbed Stella by the ear. "Come on, Stella, let's blow this dump!"

They hurried out of the bar as everyone breathed a sigh of relief.

Back at the Factory, Mr. Shadow hung up the new class schedule at the Factory. It took him a while, but he finally got it stuck to the wall with the help of three wads of grape gum. By late afternoon the gum would be covered with sugar-hungry ants.

The schedule had divided the Sticks into groups, primarily by age, and listed the class meeting times and descriptions. The three classes were described as followed:

Life Two

#1   CLASS NAME: City Secrets
        PROFESSOR: Mr. Shadow
        DESCRIPTION: Journey with Mr. Shadow through the city in search of secret passageways and quick escape routes. Learn how to turn common street items into effective and deadly weapons. CLASS TIME: One hour per day.

#2   CLASS NAME: War Strategy
        PROFESSOR: Vittles
        DESCRIPTION: Vittles will take you through the necessary strategic battle plans concerning attack situations. You will learn how to use your head and work as a team in the unfortunate event of an alley invasion. Combat moves will also be stressed. CLASS TIME: One hour per day.

#3   CLASS NAME: Waffles' Workout
        PROFESSOR: Waffles
        DESCRIPTION: To strengthen, energize, and prepare your body for the additional physical endurance needed to win a battle. Be sure to come to class well rested, and don't forget to eat breakfast. CLASS TIME: One hour per day.

MANDATORY MEETING TOMORROW AT 10 A.M. DON'T BE LATE!

The next day, everyone gathered in the rec room for the meeting. Ms. PurrPurr, the reading teacher, even took her new students out of class for the presentation. Little did they know they were about to begin Stick Bootcamp. Twinkle Toes was the only absent Stick. He

59

was happily enjoying his new home.

Everyone sat nervously on the rec room pillows and floor. After much anticipation, Mr. Shadow stepped forward.

Waffles had set up a mini-podium for him to stand behind made from an abandoned milk crate found on the sidewalk. Mr. Shadow took his position behind the crate and looked out at his audience. They seemed restless, in need of answers. A low grumble rolled through the room, making Mr. Shadow squirm in his sweater. He stood on his hind legs and placed his two front paws on the green, plastic crate. Then, like the great orator he always imagined he'd be, he waved his paw and said, "Thank you. Thank you all for coming." There was silence in the room.

"We can't hear you!" Snickers yelled from the back.

"I said, thank you for coming! Now, Mr. Sox asked me to speak today for a very important reason... *Fidel*." The crowd hissed. "Settle down, settle down," Mr. Shadow motioned. "Let's get down to business. Fidel has bothered us many times in the past, but nothing like last week's attack. He viciously took away our beloved Queen Elizabeth, an unforgivable crime. It is time for us to rise up and take action! Show Fidel once and for all that we will not sit back and take his abuse any longer!" The crowd went wild. Mr. Shadow stood proud over the wails and cries. They cheered and pounded and threw each other into the air.

Life Two

"Are we going to kill him?" shouted an angry voice from the center of the room.

"I want to do it myself! With my own teeth!" chimed another.

"Let's ransack all the alleyways!"

Mr. Shadow struggled to get the crowd back under his control, but it was no use. They were far too excited.

"Uh...excuse me, excuse me, everybody!" he screamed through the room. "Calm down! Calm down..." Just then, a trout flew and hit him in the face.

Mr. Sox was standing off to the side. He couldn't bear the unruly scene any longer. The Sticks were always emotional when it came to Fidel, especially now, but this was ridiculous. He lifted off his glasses and carefully stepped up to the podium. By now, Mr. Shadow was crouched down and hiding behind the milk crate.

As soon as Mr. Sox stepped up, one by one the Sticks grew silent, until the entire room was at a dead calm. For whatever reason, Mr. Sox could command a room far better than Mr. Shadow. Something about his presence.

Mr. Sox elegantly cleared his throat and announced, "This is not an attack! Despite what you think, we are not going to hunt down Fidel, drag him through the city and kill him."

"Why not, old man?" a bitter Stick called from

Chapter Six

the front row. The crowd gasped.

Mr. Sox looked down at the cat with angry eyes. "You, young male, will join me in the library after the meeting for a lesson on manners. Am I understood?"

Stunned by his own outburst, the cat answered, "Yes....yes, Mr. Sox. I'm sorry...."

"As I was saying," Mr. Sox continued, "we are not simply going to attack Fidel or the any of the Alleys for that matter. Remember, Sticks are peaceful cats, but we are also cautious cats. We will teach each and every one of you how to defend yourselves. That involves hard work, determination, and dedication. And yes, you are required to commit to the three classes listed on the wall."

"Awe, come on!" somebody yelled.

"We graduated already!" another cried.

Once again, the crowd got out of hand. They mumbled and grumbled with upset faces. "Hush!" Sox screamed with more energy than he knew he had. "As I was saying, you *will* attend these three classes, or you may as well no longer consider yourself a Stick. For the three new students currently enrolled in Stick School, Tuesday, Delio, and Murphy, you will continue your current classes from eight until eleven, and then begin combat school from twelve to three. Yes, you heard me right, we have named this program Combat School. Now, are there any questions?"

Several cats waved their paws high into the air. The fog forming on Mr. Sox's glasses made it difficult to see. He called up his partner, Mr. Shadow, to help with the selection. "Soot, go ahead," Mr. Shadow pointed.

"Thanks. I just wanted to know, how long will we be in class, I mean, is the session six months? Or longer?" Soot asked.

Mr. Sox leaned over the milk crate. "Unlike regular Stick School, we figure Combat School will go one full month." Everyone cheered. "However," he continued. "However, that is the *initial* estimate. If Fidel attacks during that month, or after, we will resume training at an even more intensive level. In the meantime if things are peaceful after the four weeks, you will meet once a week with your class for review." Mr. Sox leaned back and stretched his muscles.

"Thank you, Mr. Sox," Soot nodded.

Mr. Shadow combed the room for another question. Uncle Fred was jumping up and down directly in the center causing the entire place to shake. He didn't know it but he was stomping on paws and tails all around him. Everyone gave him dirty looks and lunged out of his way. Thankfully Mr. Shadow chose him for the next question. "Hey there, Mr. Sox," Uncle Fred began.

"Good morning, Uncle Fred. What is your question, son?" Mr. Sox took in a deep breath and bit his lip. Uncle Fred was known for dumb questions.

"Yeah, I was wondering if there will be a lunch break or snacks served during class, because that kinda cuts into my lunch hour, ya know?"

Chapter Six

Mr. Sox rolled his eyes, "No! There will *not* be a lunch break and there will be *no* snacks! As I said before, if you don't want to take the classes, you are no longer welcome here! That's it! Thank you!" He stepped down from the podium and headed for the library.

Mr. Shadow went on to answer more questions until everyone understood the purpose of the classes and the schedule that accompanied them. Immediately following the meeting he held another meeting just for the guards. The Factory would be stationing eight guards around the building, a number larger than ever before. Each guard would work in four-hour shifts, two shifts a day, in addition to combat school. Uncle Fred was not pleased. The Sticks that had more outside roaming freedom from their people would take the nighttime shifts, while the others would share the day patrols. The shifts would be effective immediately and no tardiness would be permitted. Anyone late would be denied fish from Roy and Yellowtail's, and would have to answer directly to Mr. Sox. Romeo and Fluffy were anxious to stand guard, though Mr. Sox told them they were still too young.

"But, Mr. Sox, we're old enough!" Fluffy pleaded. "Practically the same age Uncle Fred was when he started guarding. Why can't we?"

"Fluffy, Uncle Fred was almost six months older than you, and he's nearly three times your size," Mr. Sox explained. "I'm sorry, but you can't guard yet."

Romeo puckered his bottom lip. "But, please

Life Two

Mr. Sox, we'll do a really good job. Promise we will. Besides, Queen Elizabeth said I was ready to guard," Romeo added, shifty-eyed.

Mr. Sox dropped his jaw and leaned in close. "Romeo, I am ashamed of you. How dare you use her name like that? You know good and well that she never said such a thing." He paced in front of him. "Is that what you've learned here? Lying? Well, I'm shocked!"

Romeo burst into tears and leapt toward Mr. Sox. He sank to the ground and begged, "Please, Mr. Sox, I'm sorry! I'm sorry! You don't understand, I *have* to do something! You don't know what I'm going through! You don't know what it's like!" He collapsed at Mr. Sox's feet.

Mr. Sox changed his expression to one of concern. "I know, Romeo, I know." He lifted Romeo's weeping head gently with his paw. "My lives have seen many tragedies. I know how hard things can get, how sad they can be. You're frustrated. You're angry. You want revenge. There are other ways to get through this without putting the whole Factory in danger. You are growing fast, and you will soon be ready to guard, but for now put all your energies into Combat School and become as powerful as you can. Soon, you'll see, things will become easier. I promise." He wiped a tear from Romeo's face and helped him up.

"I hope you're right, Mr. Sox," Romeo sighed. "I hope you're right."

Chapter Seven

Fidel crawled through the city with his young students, Candle, Steak, Fish, and Big. He enjoyed taking the new Alleys under his dark spell, introducing them to a life of greed, power, and horror. *Alley Pride*, he called it. His forceful ways coaxed them under his cunning wing. One mistake, though, and bye-bye to Life One. Bait had experienced that unfortunate situation. He was only five weeks old, and it was his first real day on the streets. He was a young, impressionable kitten, and Fidel saw right off that Bait was an idiot. Nevertheless, he felt he had potential. Bait picked that first day to show just how dumb he was. When Fidel told everyone to attack a little old lady at the corner, Bait attacked his own shadow causing somewhat of a scene. He writhed and rolled around on the sidewalk, hissing and punching the concrete. He shattered two teeth trying to bite the curb. Fidel couldn't take it any longer, so he whacked him in the head with a broken hubcap knocking the life right out of him. Bait was dead instantly.

Unfortunately, Scuff, Fidel's longtime assistant, had lost his ninth life only one month earlier rather mysteriously on an elementary school playground at morning recess. With Fidel still in need of a new assistant, Bait got the news that he was appointed Scuff's successor when he awoke from his first death.

Fidel led the kittens through the haggard crowd with a fierce attitude. Bait tagged along as well for lack of anything better to do. He had two new gashes on his hind legs from a fight with another Alley over a stale piece of salami. He lost not only the tasty treat, but the fur on two of his paws and an ounce of blood.

Outside the sky was as gray as could be and looked heavy and hard. The streets were crowded with cranky people going home from a long day's work. Their heads were filled with murderous fantasies toward their bosses and hopeless dreams of moving out west. They stomped passed the smoky buildings on their way to yet another uneventful dinner. On this day not one of them took a taxi, though the city had enough to fill twenty football fields. Bait, who liked to ride on the yellow roofs, noticed right away.

"Hey boss," he said from the back of the pack. "What's wit no taxis?"

Fidel stopped and looked around. He walked

Chapter Seven

slowly up to Bait and smacked him in the head. "You dummy," he snapped. "Don't you remember? I already told you the cabbies are on strike. Don't you listen?"

Candle shyly stepped forward. "What's *strike*, Fidel?"

"Strike, my dear, is when employees aren't happy. They stop working until their bosses give them what they want. *Don't* get any ideas, Bait!"

"What do the cabbies want?" Fish asked, littering the air with the scent of rancid tuna.

"What do you *think* they want? More money! More! More! More!" Fidel regained his composure. "All right, let's keep going. You guys are boring me," he shrugged. The group headed on glaring into every eye they passed. The little Alleys had to run just to keep up with Fidel. Every time they trailed behind, Bait kicked them forward, sending them tumbling into the mix. This went on all evening, kick after kick.

Down Third Avenue, Fidel noticed something odd. Directly in front of him was an ordinary hot dog cart selling the same disgusting, old hot dogs, but underneath the tin cart there was a long, ratty, fat cat's tail. At least he hoped it was a cat's tail and not a dog's tail. It had bright orange and white stripes and wagged gently back and forth. Whoever it belonged to hummed a ghastly tune while beating the bottom of the cart like a drum. Fidel didn't recognize the tail. He turned his face down and hissed. His eyes lit up like fire as he slowly crept closer. Candle hid behind Bait and gagged from

Chapter Seven

the pungent odor oozing from his pores.

"Who's dat, boss?" Bait yelled.

Fidel whipped his head around and snarled, "Shut up, you idiot!" He went back to his prowl. He stepped closer and closer, while the hot dog vender continued to pour mounds of cheese and relish onto his wienies.

Fidel crept right up to the dangling tail. Only inches away, he crouched down in attack mode practically breathing onto the tail itself. Fidel raised his left paw and flexed his sharp nails. Candle shut her eyes as Fidel sent his paw crashing down, piercing the skin. Instantly, the tail's owner yelped and wailed louder than anything. From the sting of the attack it flew up hitting the underside of the hot dog cart knocking over tubs of ketchup and mustard. The way his cart was shaking and rattling, the hot dog man thought there was an earthquake. The mystery animal squirmed to get out. The more it tried, the more entangled it got, so much, in fact, that the cart went sailing down the street with the cat attached beneath. The hot dog man screamed and ran after it. Grabbing onto the back, he tried to stop it, but because of a slight decline in the road, the cart picked up speed and soared down the street spitting hot dogs all over the sidewalks.

The wiener man flung himself as hard as he could, landing on top of the cart. Hot cheese splattered all over his head, and his feet stuck in the hot dog oven. Juicy pickles whipped from their jar, smacking people in the face as they dashed out of the way.

For a block the runaway cart raced downhill. The man screamed the whole way. "Watch out! Run for your lives!" Then, as the cart approached a particularly high curb and a particularly heavy woman, its wheels planted into the curb flipping the cart upside-down and into the air. The cart, the hot dog vendor, and mounds of onions landed flat on the fat lady. Rats, mice, and other Alleys came scurrying up for the free dinner, while the problem cat lay shivering where the cart once stood. His orange and white stripes wrapped around his enormous body like a candy cane. He was not just fat, but huge like a dog, three times as big as Uncle Fred. His gritty tongue hung low from his mouth, and his eyes were crossed. One ear was incredibly bigger than the other, and he had no whiskers on his left side. When he breathed, his nostrils flared like two big balloons. Fidel grabbed his tail.

"Ouch! Ouch!" the cat wailed, holding onto his sore tail.

"Who are you, and why were you hiding under that hot dog cart? Are you a Stick spy?" Fidel screamed under the haze of a blinking street lamp.

"Huh?" the confused cat answered.

"You heard him, buster!" Bait chimed in.

"Shut up, Bait!" Fidel barked. "You heard me, are you a spy?"

The cat struggled to knock the blur out of his eyes. He was seeing four Fidels swirling in front of him.

Chapter Seven

"I'm no spy. I'm a Cheeseburger."

"You're a what?" Fidel asked snippy.

"I said I'm Cheeseburger. Pleased to meet you." He stuck out his paw to shake Fidel's. Suddenly, he fell flat on his face and started to snore obnoxiously.

Fidel once again plunged his paw into Cheeseburger's tail. Cheeseburger shot up off the sidewalk and smashed into the neon sign at Hank's Donut and Sock Shop. Cheeseburger's body sizzled and quivered finally falling back to the concrete.

"This guy's a freak. Let's get out of here!" Fidel announced. The Alleys walked away as the hotdog vendor and the fat lady struggled to their feet. They'd be shaken, not to mention smelly, for the rest of the day, but fine nonetheless.

The Alleys started on their way, stepping over Cheeseburger, except for Bait who stepped right on his tail for one final scream.

Fidel and his followers had only taken a few steps when dogs were spotted coming around the corner. Bull, the leader, was leading the pack followed by a stream of nasty, drooling hounds. The kittens started screaming and shrieking in Fidel's ears. He shoved them away with a hiss.

"Let's hide!" Candle shrieked.

"I can take 'em!" Fish said in his fiercest kitty voice.

Fidel stood firm. "Shut up!" he yelled. "Now, here's what we are going to do. Bait, you hide behind that mailbox and when I say go you..."

While Fidel explained his attack plan, Bull snuck up behind him gritting his stained teeth. Bait tried to get Fidel's attention. He pointed and waved his paw in the direction of the dog. Finally Fidel acknowledged his nervous behavior. "What is it already, Bait?"

"Dogs!!" he exploded.

Just then, Bull growled loud enough for the whole city to hear. Hank locked his Donut and Sock shop door fast. Bull's teeth were green and decayed, his fur gooey and matted. Candle immediately hid under an old lady's dress, but the others hissed their little hearts out. Bait stuck out his bottom jaw, huffed twice and went charging for the dogs. He smashed headfirst into one of the larger mutts, getting knocked out cold. The dog didn't even flinch. Fidel inhaled as hard as he could, puffing himself up to nearly twice his size. His fur stood straight up on end and his claws nearly dug right into the cement. At last he was face to face with the notorious leader of the dogs. The reality of death flashed through his mind. He knew he could take on Bull himself, but what about that brick wall of dogs behind him? It didn't matter now. Bull was his target.

The two animals faced each other nose to nose, stinging the other with nasty breath. Fidel arched his back as high as he could, forming a perfect half circle. He was ready to pounce. But as he made his move, the rest of the dogs encircled him, shielding him from Bull. Fidel hissed and growled at the dogs, but they towered over him like dark clouds. Fish, Steak, and Big bit and tugged at the dogs' huge tails, hanging on like little pesky Christmas ornaments. Fish clenched his teeth onto one of the Dobermans. The dog lifted him up with his tail and swung him into a newspaper rack. Bait still lay drooling on the concrete.

Fidel wildly scrambled for a way to escape the circle of dogs. He was trapped, and he knew it. Suddenly, the dogs closed in tighter all around him. He twisted and shifted his body in every direction. As the dogs growled, they oozed thick globs of mucus through their rows of sharp, devilish teeth. For the first time Fidel was scared, really scared. His heart pounded faster than ever before. He spotted Bull staring him down atop of one of the dog's heads. He howled twice and gave Fidel a sinister stare. Bull leapt up, stuck out his thick claws and soared down in Fidel's direction. Fidel quickly prepared himself mentally for a fight, when suddenly, out of nowhere, charged Cheeseburger. He rammed the dogs like a bowling ball, including Bull, shooting them off in different directions. They stumbled for a moment, shaking their heads from the blow. Their vision was blurry and hazy.

Fidel knew he had no time to waste. Immediately he shouted to his crew, "Let's go! Follow me!" They shot off down the street weaving in and out of all the people. Candle tried her best to keep up, though she couldn't run very fast and was trailing far behind. Cheeseburger looked over his shoulder and saw her struggling. He immediately dashed back, took her in his mouth and flung her on his back. He ran off with a roar as Candle held tightly to the fur on his neck. She closed her eyes tightly and prayed with all her might.

Back at the Donut and Sock Shop, Hank had come out with a broom to swat at the dogs. "Get outta here, ya dumb mutts!" he shouted. "Get away! You hear me? Get away from my store! And stay away!"

The big tough dogs yelped and whined. All, that is, but one. Bull. He could be seen storming after Fidel, getting closer and closer. Fidel could sense Bull's hot breath on his tail as he approached fast. Up ahead he knew of a high wooden fence at the end of an alley. "This way!" Fidel screamed to his cats as he raced into the alley and heaved himself over it. The others did the same. When Cheeseburger jumped, his big body tumbled and wobbled, just barely reaching the top. He hung onto the rusty wood as Candle hung onto him. Bull spotted them as he rounded the corner into the alley. Cheeseburger managed to pull himself up with all his might finally flinging himself over the fence. As he did, Candle lost her balance and fell to the alley floor. Fidel screamed from the other side, "Grab her! We can't lose her!"

But it was too late. Bull's piercing eyes met with Candle's. She let out a cry and shivered herself into a tiny ball. Bull smirked and lunged high into the air. Just as he did Cheeseburger's paw suddenly punched through one of the fence slats and grabbed Candle from the other side. He yanked her through the tiny opening just as Bull came crashing down banging his head into the fence. The stunned dog became enraged. He tried to wedge himself through the hole, but it was no use. It was too small, even for him. Standing there alone in the alley, he cursed and swatted at a swarm of flies buzzing around his sweaty head. After a few minutes he gave up and left.

On the other side of the fence, Fidel and the rest of the Alleys were safe. Relieved, Fidel breathed heavily. Candle was hurt but would be all right. Cheeseburger opened his mouth like he was about to say something. "What is it?" Fidel asked.

Just then, a huge fur ball erupted out of Cheeseburger's mouth and squashed onto the ground. "Uh...sorry," he apologized. "That always happens when I'm nervous."

"Now you're nervous? *Now* you're nervous?" Fidel snapped. "You mean you weren't nervous before?"

"Duh, I guess not. I mean, it was all so fast, y'know?" he answered as yet another yucky fur ball flung from his mouth. He smiled a dumb smile and shrugged his shoulders.

"Bait! Where's Bait?" Fidel asked annoyed. "Where the hell is Bait?"

All of a sudden Bait's battered face emerged from the top of the fence. "Hey, guys," he slurred. Like a limp rag, his swollen body slid down the side of the fence

Life Two

and fell to the ground. "Zzzzzzzzzz," he snored.

Fidel rolled his eyes then turned to Cheeseburger. "So, what's with you anyway, *Cheeseburger*?"

Cheeseburger looked around. "Me?"

"Yeah, you, dummy! Look, I'd like to make you a deal. Sure, you're a moron, but you're tough too. I could use a guy like you. Whadaya say?"

Cheeseburger blushed. "Gosh, no one's ever said that to me before." A lone tear streamed down his funny face. "Yes! I'll do it! I'll do it!" He lunged forward to give Fidel a hug. Fidel swatted at him away and stepped back just in the nick of time as Cheeseburger threw up one more ball of fur.

Chapter Eight

Throughout the week, Combat School was well under way. Mr. Shadow was heavy into his excitingly detailed lectures on secrets of the city, Vittles terrified everyone with his war strategies, and Waffles had everyone pumping up. Despite the rigorous schedule, all cats attended, Calvin being the only consistent late arrival. His beauty rest took a higher priority. Mr. Sox made him stay and clean out the female's litter box as punishment. He would never look at another female the same way again.

On Monday Romeo sat attentively in Mr. Shadow's noontime class. Mr. Shadow taught a grueling five sessions a day leaving little time for himself or his guard duty shifts. Romeo's class was filled with all his old chums from Stick School; Darla, Tabitha, Calvin, Fluffy, Snickers, Twinkle Toes, and even Uncle Fred, among several others, including the three newest Sticks. They used the Thinking Room as their classroom.

"Now, before I go," Mr. Shadow said. "Remember what I taught you about rubber bands. You should always have one wrapped around your paw. They make excellent weapons. One little fling and you could take somebody's eye right out of its socket."

"Gross!" Darla gagged. "Please, Mr. Shadow, don't say another word about it." She clutched her stomach.

"I'll have none of that," Mr. Shadow warned. "But I do expect to see all of you tomorrow with a rubber band. That is your homework. And I am warning you, no flicking them at me! War preparations are serious business!" He added threateningly. "Then we will go out into the streets and practice shooting them at small rats and mice. The best students will get to eat the ones we catch." Everyone's face lit up, especially Snickers who was growing hungrier by the minute. "That's all for today. Until tomorrow."

All the students took a quick stretch before heading to Vittles' next class in the art room. Vittles pushed all the art tables aside allowing ample room for his Battle Strategy Workshop. Before going in Snickers prowled around for anything with legs.

"Go ahead, I'll catch up," Snickers said as everyone rushed by him. "I'll be right there." He quickly ran to the corner of the building where he often spotted rodents. Snickers grinned at the streams of spider webs

Chapter Eight

hanging from the rafters. Half-eaten moths and flies stuck to the thicker webs. He walked through them allowing each sticky strand to drift across his face. As he took a breath one of them shot up his nose. Snickers quickly sneezed it out.

High atop this arachnid masterpiece was Octavian, the spider. He stared down at Snickers from his web hardly fearing for his life. He had spent many days watching the stupid cat but never once fell victim to his hearty appetite. Again Snickers caught sight of Octavian and began feverously lunging at the spider. Octavian just sat there perched on his eight feet, resting his head on one of his legs. He grimaced at Snickers. Winded and unsuccessful, Snickers gave up and went to class. Sadly, he missed the shrimp Vittles had just handed out to all his students. Romeo ate the last one.

"How was I supposed to know you wanted a shrimp?" Romeo nagged picking a morsel from between his two front teeth.

"What do you mean? Of course you knew I'd wanted a shrimp. Duh," Snickers whined, bits of drool dribbling from his mouth. "Why didn't you save me one?"

"I thought you were going to eat that spider," Romeo pointed out.

"Yeah, well, I didn't want him. He's ugly."

Octavian heard him from his web and shook his head.

Snickers walked up to Vittles and asked

innocently, "Will there be more shrimp tomorrow?"

"No," Vittles said, and turned around. "In fact, there won't be any shrimp for a long time."

"Why not?" Darla asked, butting into the conversation.

"Because Roy and Yellowtail can't get any fish until the fish markets open again."

"Why are they closed?" Tabitha asked.

"In support of the striking fishermen who are demanding higher wages. They get paid next to nothing for spending their days on those murky, rough waters."

"Gosh," Fluffy interrupted. "It seems like a lot of the people are out on these strikes lately. Have you noticed that the buses are overflowing with people?"

Vittles answered, "Yes, it's because the cab drivers are on strike too, along with the fishermen and the phone company operators. It seems everybody wants more money."

"Well, I want some shrimp!" Snickers shouted.

"Good luck. You're better off trying for that sneaky spider again," Vittles chuckled.

Snickers stuck his nose high in the air. "Humph."

"All right, all right," Vittles said. "It's time to get to work. Everybody find a place to sit. Tuesday, Delio, and Murphy, why don't you sit up front where you can see better."

The three little kittens scurried their way to the front of the class. Delio stepped right in fur ball someone selfishly left behind. He could feel it squish beneath his paw. The whole morning he pretended the icky goo wasn't there, although it unfortunately was.

"Thank you all for being on time," Vittles announced. "Especially *you*, Calvin."

Calvin rolled his eyes.

"Today we are going to work in groups of five," Vittles explained in a serious tone as he paced at the front of the room. "Now, there are three different attack plans you must master. This is *very* important, so please pay *close* attention."

Of course, not many did. Most of the Sticks in the back sat daydreaming or twiddling their paws. They didn't see the point to all these classes. Sure, everyone was still on edge, yet they refused to admit to the possibility of a full scale war looming in their future. Of course, they attended their classes because they had to, but their minds were elsewhere. Romeo and Fluffy, however, always sat at complete attention. A teacher's dream.

"Imagine that you and your buddies are taking an afternoon jaunt through the city," Vittles began, "when an uninvited Alley decides to join your group. Maybe he hisses at you, maybe he jets out his claws and tries to scratch you!" Vittles shouted through the room, prowling low to the ground. "Or maybe he's stalking you, planning a slow and painful death in which you will lay in your own blood at the back of some abandoned alley, awaiting your next death!"

They all sat up straight.

Life Two

"Now that I have your attention, you should *not* be strolling around town until everything cools off, see? But for the sake of argument, let's say you're out there." Vittles hunched over and walked sneakily around the room. "Pretend an Alley cat *is* stalking you, only you and your friends don't know it, see. He slithers up behind you, following you very closely. Suddenly, he slyly signals to his friends who are *meaner* and *uglier* and *fiercer* than him!" Tuesday, Delio, and Murphy all covered their eyes and trembled. Darla ran to the litteroom, and Tabitha moved in closer to Romeo. "Then, when you and your friends walk past the alleyway, they make their move. They know they've *got* you. One pounces out of nowhere, landing directly in front of you. Out comes another! And another! They corner you and hiss you into the shadows where they can do whatever they want. There's no telling how many Alleys will be waiting, maybe even...Fidel!"

"Ahhh!!" everyone gasped. Tabitha jumped into Romeo's lap. Romeo blushed beneath his fur.

Vittles circled the cats making creepy faces and sounds.

"What should we do?" Uncle Fred whined.

"That, my friend, is the question we have to answer today. What do you do?" Vittles pondered. "Every Stick plays an important role in battle. When we finish our discussion here, we will be going out into the hallway to practice our strategies. Some of you will have to play the part of the Alleys."

"Me! Me! Me!" Snickers waved. "I want to be an

Alley! I want to be an Alley!"

"We'll see. Anyway," he continued. "As I said, everyone plays a crucial role."

Vittles took great pride that morning teaching the young Sticks the ways of the streets. By the end of the hour, each one had been introduced to such classic strategies as Battle Plans X and Z, Operation Rain Drop, Jaw Cruncher, The Eye Squeeze, the newly renovated Knock-Knock Zoink-Splat, and the infamous Situation Death.

"These will prepare your minds before you can sink into panic mode, then it's too late. Your fur shoots up like needles, and you allow your bodies to be mangled by the Alleys. You *will* be fierce! You *will* be brave! You *will* win!" he echoed, each time getting louder and louder. "You will practice over and over, and over and over, until the plans become engrained in your meek, little skulls! Am I understood?"

"What if the Alleys have a plan too? What if it's a better plan than ours?" asked Maybelle from behind her long, curly eyelashes.

Vittles paced back and forth letting his heavy tail drag behind him. "Good question, Maybelle," he answered. "See, we have to remember that no matter how hard we train, how intensively we plan and practice, there's *always* the possibility that the Alleys will outsmart us. Remember, they have advantages we don't. They live on the streets. They don't have easy lives. They're raised on violence and blood! They're tough, and they know we know it. But, where does that leave us? Should we give in and not even try?"

"No!" everyone shouted.

"Should we allow ourselves to become victims again and again?"

"No!" they said louder.

"Should we send Fidel the message that he is king, and we are nothing but his lowly servants ready and willing to lick his grubby paws?"

"No way!" they screamed, stirring into an uproar.

"Then let's show them who we are and stand up for ourselves!" Vittles chimed above the crowd."

"Yeah!" the class cheered.

Vittles waved his paws and yelled, "Now, settle down, settle down, everybody! Yes, the Alleys are tough and cruel and just plain mean, but we have a better weapon. Does anybody know what that is?"

Everyone looked at Vittles with a blank stare.

"We have brains," Vittles said. "We are smart," he puffed, pointing at his head. *"That* my friends, is our most prized weapon. Now, let's get to work!"

The next and last hour of the day was spent at Waffles' Workout. Though painful and sweaty, everyone liked this class best. Waffles had music and water and napkins. The music was played by Sticks that had made some rudimentary instruments from junk around the Factory. Umbrella pieces made surprisingly interesting noises.

Chapter Eight

"All right, you weaklings," Waffles scowled. "Do ten laps around the room, and then we'll begin our exercises. Let's move! Hey, where's Uncle Fred? He better not be ditching!"

"No," Soot replied urgently. "He's got guard duty."

"Oh," Waffles mumbled.

The workout was held in the library because of its large size, which meant Mr. Sox had to find a new place to read, but he was up to the sacrifice.

Waffles laid out a running track by using dozens of library books as markers. Between the two oval shaped rows of books was nearly five feet of jogging space. Waffles immediately noticed Calvin sluggishly stumbling around the room, kicking books out of his way. "Calvin! Pick up the pace and stop lagging!"

"Why don't you?" Calvin mumbled.

"Excuse me?" Waffles approached. "What did you *say*, boy?" He stepped closer, quickly erasing the smirk from Calvin's face. Waffles was a hefty, muscular cat just like his brother, Vittles. He had a frighteningly low voice and eyes that could sting. Startled, Calvin dashed around the track faster than ever.

"I thought so," said Waffles, backing away.

Romeo was a fast runner, maybe even the fastest. His little black and gray legs raced through the room, pounding against the floor like buffalo. Such skill would certainly be useful in the bustling city. He finished his ten laps in no time. Sweaty and worn out, he quickly went to one of the three bowls of cool water.

"Save some for us!" Snickers called. He was only on his third lap, though already out of breath. His tubby body gurgled and burbled and bounced against his stubby legs.

Everyone bumbled around the track, panting, huffing, and puffing out of breath. The last lap was sluggish at best, but somehow everyone survived, except one.

"Get a load of Snickers!" Delio wheezed. "He's not going to make it!"

"Shut up, new guy! Go home to your puppy dog!" Snickers snapped with his last ounce of energy. Sadly, he knew Delio was right. Everybody else was heading for the water bowls. Waffles rolled his eyes. Other Sticks were laughing or pointing, while some puffed out their cheeks imitating his fat form. As Snickers struggled along the track, he started to cry.

Romeo stepped forward and asked Waffles a question. "Uh...shouldn't we get started? There's not much time left." He gave Waffles a wink and mouthed the word *please*.

Waffles got Romeo's message. "Oh, all right. Snickers, get over here. You can stop running," he said.

Snickers came over to the others, completely out of breath. "Thanks, man," he whispered, spraying sweat all over Romeo's shiny fur.

Snickers lumbered over to the water bowls, knocked little Murphy out of the way and dove right into the water headfirst. Murphy lay dumbfounded in a puddle on the floor. "Wha...what happened?" he slurred.

Snickers chuckled and kicked water all over the place. Everyone yelled at him and ran to the other side of the room. Some of the water hit the books sending Waffles into a nasty rage. "Snickers, get out of there, now!" he roared. "Now!"

Snickers shot out of the bowl like a bat and stood at perfect attention, dripping everyone's drinking water onto the wooden floor. Waffles threw him a stack of paper towels and ordered him to clean up. "The rest of you," he went on, "stand still on all fours. I'm going to place a big, heavy open book on your backs. Then, you will begin a series of leg bends, all four legs! Do you hear me?"

"Yes," the cats mumbled unenthusiastically.

Waffles put a book on everyone's back. They were heavy like he said. Romeo turned his head around and noticed that his book was about ghosts. There was a picture of a gray floating head on the cover. Fluffy had one about worms, and Twinkle Toes had something written in Japanese. When all were ready, Waffles began. "Okay, bend at the knees, then stand up slowly. One, two, three, four."

All the Sticks crouched down and stood up to the beat of Waffles' counting. It was hard. Their little muscles burned inside their tiny legs. By the third round, the book pages were becoming damp and smelly from

Life Two

their sweat. Snickers collapsed under the weight of his book. Waffles finally took it away and bitterly replaced it with a small magazine.

After class ended Mr. Sox came around to see how everyone was doing. He found them all back in the rec room. Snickers had passed out. Sprawled across the biggest, comfiest pillow, he snored loudly.

"Why is Snickers so tired?" Mr. Sox asked. "And look at how he drools!"

Snickers' tongue was hanging out dripping drool onto the pillow.

"He's gross!" Tuesday squirmed. She and Tabitha shared a blue velvet pillow, while Romeo and Twinkle Toes sat nearby on the homemade couch. They looked like big, floppy stuffed animals as they cooled off from their rigorous workout. Some cats had already gone home. Suddenly Soot came running in from his guard shift looking scared and shaken.

"What is it?" Maybelle cried. "Is everything all right?"

"Is it Fidel?" Romeo shuddered.

Soot stepped forward in a panic, "Come quick! Follow me!"

With that, everyone leapt from their pillows and dashed outside following Soot. Vittles, who was guarding the front entrance, pointed to his left. "Look!" he shouted. Every little Stick head turned and immediately saw the problem. It was Uncle Fred. He was stuck high up in an old, withered tree near the end of the building where no one ever went. The tree had no pretty leaves, or anything green at all. Rather, it was a ladder of dead branches, abandoned, crumpled bird nests, and prickly edges. Reaching nearly three stories high, it shaded the weeds and pot holes beneath it. Uncle Fred clung with all his might atop the highest branch, shaking like the leaves it didn't have.

"Help!" he cried. "Get me down from here! I want my momma!"

They couldn't believe their eyes.

"What are you doing up there?" Romeo hollered.

"What?" Uncle Fred bellowed. "Who said that?"

Mr. Sox came rushing out of the building. He had heard the news and was completely befuddled. "What is that darn cat up to?" He mumbled to himself.

Tabitha ran up to him. "Mr. Sox, what are we going to do?"

Mr. Sox paced back and forth in front of the crowd of Sticks. He put his glasses on, took them off then put them back on again. Finally, he spoke. "Okay, here's the plan. First of all, Soot, cover your station and Uncle Fred's. We don't want any *surprise* visitors slipping by us."

"Got it!" Soot saluted returning to his post.

"Now, this next part will be tricky. We have no way of getting him down from there ourselves. We're going to need some outside help," Mr. Sox explained.

Life Two

"Let me think, I will need about three, no, four of you."

Everyone's paws shot straight up into the air, waving like crazy. Romeo and Fluffy jumped up and down right in front of Mr. Sox's face.

"All right, males, all right," Mr. Sox chuckled. "You two can help."

"Yeah!" Fluffy yelled, giving Romeo a high-five.

"Delio and Murphy, you're too little for this. How about Twinkle Toes and Tabitha? Step forward please." Delio and Murphy rolled their disappointed eyes.

"Help!" Uncle Fred wailed again from his sky perch.

"Oh, shut up! Help is on the way!" Tabitha lashed out.

Mr. Sox gathered his four helpers into a huddle. He whispered a secret plan to them as he pointed to the old phone booth across the street. It stood in front of Scissor Bob's Barber Shop. A giant pair of rusty scissors hung from the door as advertising. People hardly ever used that phone. No one hardly ever went to Scissor Bob's either.

Mr. Sox whispered something secret to Twinkle Toes then ordered him to run into the Factory. He did and quickly returned with two shiny objects. They were two quarters Mr. Sox had been saving for an emergency. It was a rule that all Sticks were required to

Chapter Eight

immediately turn in any coins they found. It happened a lot. The Factory already had two dollars and forty-three cents. Mr. Sox kept the money hidden away in a secret drawer. Only he, and now Twinkle Toes, knew of its whereabouts.

The others watched anxiously as Uncle Fred whined and whimpered from up high. Then, Mr. Sox repeated the plan, opened his mouth and slowly said, "One, two, three...go!"

The four Sticks darted across the street, Romeo clutching the coins in his teeth. They headed for the phone. Four, foggy, glass walls, cracked and scribbled with graffiti surrounded it. The door to the booth was closed tight. Fluffy tried to pry it open but quickly realized he wasn't strong enough. Teamwork would be called for. All four cats huffed and puffed and together managed to slide the door open, pulling a few muscles in the process.

Tabitha was stationed as a lookout while the other three quickly scrambled inside the booth. They could see Mr. Sox waiting nervously across the street. The wind started to pick up speed knocking Uncle Fred back and forth. Mr. Sox motioned for them to hurry. Inside, Romeo jumped onto the tiny ledge beneath the phone where an expired phone book dangled on a chain and swayed. Fluffy sprung up and sat next to Romeo.

"What do I do? What do I do?" Romeo panicked, knocking some empty spider webs out of his way.

Life Two

"Put the quarters in, dummy!" Fluffy screamed. "And don't forget to throw down the receiver, like Mr. Sox said!"

"That's *your* job!" Romeo snapped.

"Oh, yeah."

Romeo gripped the quarters in his paw and searched for the hole in the phone, getting his paw stuck on some yucky taffy. "Ah, here it is!" Romeo managed to stuff one quarter into the slot, but the other fell and rolled in tiny circles on the floor. "Get it, Twinkle Toes! Quick!" he yelled.

"Hurry!" Tabitha wailed, sticking her head into the booth. "I see *people* coming this way!"

Twinkle Toes twisted around in the tiny booth finally finding the shiny quarter on the ground. He tossed it back up to Romeo, hitting him in the eye. It fell to the ground again.

"Ouch!" Romeo screamed. "Watch where you're throwing next time!" Twinkle Toes tried again.

Finally Romeo caught it on the third throw and successfully slid the quarter into the phone slot. "Hurray!" he cheered.

Fluffy quickly flung the black plastic receiver down to Twinkle Toes. As it fell, Twinkle leapt up to catch it. However, it bounced off his head knocking him dizzy. He crashed to the floor like a sack of sugar. Out cold. "Come on, guys!" Tabitha yelled again. "They're coming! The people are coming!"

In a frantic move, Fluffy pulled on the phone

Chapter Eight

cord bringing the receiver up to his face. "Dial!" he roared to Romeo. Romeo feverishly dialed the three sacred numbers: 9-1-1.

Now in most cities, a call like this would be free, but because of some bizarre wage disputes at the phone company, all calls, even emergency ones, were two quarters. Shameful.

Fluffy heard the phone ringing on the other end. His heart was pounding in his chest. Never before had he tried to talk to a human. Technically, they were never allowed to, the ultimate sin. However, exceptions were made in very rare cases such as these. Fluffy would have to scream as loud as he could for the emergency operator to hear him at all.

"Faster!" Tabitha hollered. "Faster!" Across the street the Sticks were jumping nervously up and down. Fluffy heard someone answer the phone.

"Emergency 9-1-1," the voice said clearly.

Fluffy heaved in a huge mouthful of air and hollered, "Come for the cat in the big tree on 54th and 13th!"

"Huh?" the operator asked. "You'll have to speak louder."

"Come for the cat in the big tree on 54th and 13th!" he thundered again.

"The big tree on 54th and 13th? I'll send someone right away, ma'am...uh, sir."

Click.

Romeo and Fluffy jumped down and

Life Two

immediately started shaking Twinkle Toes awake. The people, who were only steps away, pointed at the funny cats in the phone booth. "Come on, Toes!" Romeo slapped. "Snap out of it!"

"Huh? Wha...?" Twinkle Toes slurred.

"Get up!" Romeo screeched, practically piercing his eardrums. Twinkle Toes shot up like a cannon, dazed and bewildered. He banged his head with a hard thud on the glass wall, nearly shattering it to bits. Then Romeo slapped him in the face repeatedly to keep him from slipping back into his groggy state. Tabitha stood near the open door and waved everybody out of the booth.

"Go! Go! Go!" she roared.

They raced out and ran across the street, collapsing on the sidewalk. As Romeo ran, his taffy covered paw stuck to the concrete with each hurried leap. The other Sticks waited with baited breath.

"Well?" Mr. Sox asked. "What happened over there? Did it work?"

Romeo took a deep breath. "The lady answered," he said. "They're coming! They should be here soon!"

"Hang on, Uncle Fred!" Tabitha called in her loudest voice. "It won't be long now!"

Above, Uncle Fred wagged his tail, still clutching onto the same rickety branch. Because of all his wiggling, some twigs had scratched his butt up pretty good.

"I hear them!" Tuesday leaped as she heard the sirens careening up the street. Sure enough,

Chapter Eight

the emergency vehicles zoomed up to the Factory, shamelessly splashing mud and gook on anyone and anything in their path. Bug bits lined the tires and splattered across the front windshield. Soot watched the whole saga unfold from behind a large bush. He would later tell this story:

"So the big fire truck drove up really fast. They see Uncle Fred high in that tree. Boy, did he look pathetic, like a little baby. The main fireman, I guess, took out this huge ladder and stuck it next to the tree. He climbed up real slow and tried to grab Uncle Fred, only he kept slipping out of his hands because he was so sweaty. So anyway, he finally grabs him by the neck, Uncle Fred kicking and meowing, and just drops him onto the sidewalk like a lump. The fire guy dusted all the dirt off his hands. I saw him looking around for the person who made the phone call, but I guess he gave up. He had a weird look on his face, like he was mad or something. Then he drove away. The lights were really cool!"

After the sirens sped out of sight, Uncle Fred stumbled into the rec room and plopped onto a big pillow. He was mangled and cold and covered in mud. Adrenalin still pumped through his body, and he shivered endlessly. The scrapes on his butt made him walk funny.

"Well?" Fluffy asked. "What happened?"

"I was in the tree! You know that!" Uncle Fred whined.

Life Two

"But why? How'd you get up there?" Romeo asked.

Uncle Fred looked at him with ashamed eyes and confessed, "I thought I saw something. I thought it might be an Alley! So I climbed the tree to get a better look." His mouth turned to a frown.

Mr. Sox stepped forward. "What *did* you see, son? Was it an Alley?"

"No."

"Well, what was it?" he asked again.

"Was it a dead animal, all disgusting with its eyes bugged out and green things hanging from its nose?" Snickers grilled.

"No, it was a *dnlguhdx,*" Uncle Fred mumbled.

"What?"

"A donut box," he said. "It was a donut box, all right! I thought it looked like an Alley, so there!"

They all laughed until their bellies burned. Could he have mistaken an old pink box for an Alley cat? No one could believe he was actually that stupid. Purely dumbfounded, they pulled his whiskers, flicked his ears and threw bark at his nose. Uncle Fred bawled until it hurt. He didn't know what was worse, the cruel, humiliating teasing or the stinging scrapes all over his rump. Mr. Sox soon made everyone go home and let poor, embarrassed Uncle Fred do the same.

"Uncle Fred," Mr. Sox began. "I'll walk you home, son, but I want to establish a new rule for you."

Chapter Eight

"What is it, Mr. Sox?"

"If you *ever* think you see an Alley again, get one of the other guards before you do anything! Don't handle it yourself. Understood?"

"Yes, Mr. Sox. I understand."

"Good, I'll let the other guards know. Now, let's get you home." Together, the two sticks journeyed on, Uncle Fred whimpering the entire way.

Chapter Nine

Fidel gulped down his fourth beer at Smelly's Bar over the glow of his bug jar. He closed his eyes and allowed the bitter ale to sink down to his belly. His genius plan against the pesky Sticks was mere steps away from completion. "Bait!" he snarled. "Will we be ready to strike tonight? You'd *better* say yes!"

Bait had just stepped into the bar, barely halfway though the door when he heard Fidel's bluster. His body twitched nervously, and he said, "Sure, boss. Yeah, we can go in tonight. Them Sticks have guards all over da place, but I thinks I found a good spot we can go."

"What do you mean, they're *all* over the place?" Fidel howled knocking his empty beer glass to the floor. "I thought you said everything was fine! You didn't *lie* to me, did you, Bait? Because if you did-- "

Chapter Nine

"No, no, Fidel," Bait interrupted. "Really, it's going to work. I found just the perfect place to go in. Trust me. It's gonna work. Them dummies won't know what hit 'em."

"Good, Bait, good," Fidel said, calming down and gritting his teeth. He turned around to look at his team of rabble-rousers. "Clank, Fink, Mustard, is the *tree* ready?" They looked at each other and nodded their heads. Fidel rubbed his front paws together and moaned with a sinister stare. "Be forewarned, *Sticks*, Fidel is coming!" He swatted Bait out of his way and stormed out of the bar with a ghoulish laugh. The others felt queasy as they watched him leave.

Back at the Factory the Sticks were winding down from a long day at class. It was late Friday afternoon, and evening was quickly approaching. As a safety precaution, all Sticks went home by five o'clock to avoid the dark streets. The night guards would be starting their shift. Some of them, like Waffles, had just completed their teaching duties. Uncle Fred was starting to get used to his crowded schedule of classes and guard duty. His people didn't notice that he was coming in so late. Even though the Alley panic was thick in the night air, Uncle Fred didn't mind the solitary walk home. He promised Mr. Sox he'd always be careful, and sometimes he even slept at the Factory when the weather was particularly bad.

Uncle Fred was scheduled to work all weekend long, as he did most weekends. Unlike some of the

Life Two

others, he quite enjoyed guard duty. Since the tree incident, he was very careful not to do anything stupid. He stood solid and dignified like a soldier at his post. Yet somehow, he was dorky at the same time. Some of the other guards would imitate Uncle Fred's stiff posture when he wasn't looking. They stuck out their bellies and clenched their toes together, swatting at flies and rigidly staring at the sky. Uncle Fred was quickly becoming the butt of all their jokes. Still, he desperately wanted to prove to Mr. Sox and the others that he was a responsible, capable guard worthy of respect and admiration. He wanted to make them proud.

Fred's station was to the far south corner of the building between two large, old trees, one having been the scene of his recent embarrassment. The quiet corner faced an empty lot on either side. It was scattered with torn clothes, abandoned toys, and broken beer bottles. Down the street stood good old Scissor Bob's, Tiffany's House of Zippers, Jimmy Jack's At Home Sausage Fillings, and Aunt Martha's Orphanage. Most of the stores and businesses to the south side of the block disappeared after the umbrella fire. The meager few remaining were not exactly a paradise to view.

Uncle Fred stepped out at five o'clock sharp and relieved Mr. Shadow from his shift. "Okay, Mr. Shadow," he said puffing out his chest. "Go relax. I'm here and in charge."

Mr. Shadow quivered at the sound of those

Chapter Nine

words. He continued with hesitation. "All right, Uncle Fred, now remember, if you suspect any Alleys, any at all..."

"I know, I know, go find somebody to help me. I remember," Uncle Fred quickly responded.

"Good," Mr. Shadow sighed. "If there are any problems, come inside. Several of us are staying for a six o'clock meeting, so please let us know if you need any help."

"Don't worry about a thing," Uncle Fred said again. "No Alley is going to get by this guy." He stood up tall and sucked in as much air he could until his chest pumped up like a shiny balloon.

Mr. Shadow shook his head and disappeared around the corner. Uncle Fred slithered slowly back and forth along the wall, guarding it like a detective on a special secret mission. He snuck up to the tree branches pretending they were bad guys and attacked them with his laser-powered paws. He ended the scenario by doing a dumb little dance as he plucked the splinters out of the pads on his feet.

The night seemed calm, and Uncle Fred quickly became tired of his detective game. With only a sliver of a moon in the sky, it was quite dark, and the night sounds came alive. Crickets, mice, strange moans and groans echoed through the air. The wind seemed to howl louder at night, and the rain clouds teased Uncle Fred mercilessly. He shivered in the cold, his sleepy eyes trying to stay peeled for action. Suddenly, he heard a strange, creaky, squeaky sound, like an old, forgotten bicycle. It was coming from around the corner. Uncle Fred froze. His body began to shoot beads of sweat through his heavy fur. Remembering his promise to Mr. Sox, he slinked to the corner, which was still his terrain.

Uncle Fred decided he had better take a quick look before telling the others about it. They would be awfully mad if he interrupted their meeting on just a crazy hunch. Before he peeked around the edge of the building, the noise got louder, then suddenly stopped.

He continued to creep around the corner, slower and slower, his eyes bugging out. Then he saw it! The startling shape of a large object! In the dark it looked like a massive monster, tall and fierce, ten cats high. Uncle Fred trembled and twitched; yet something inside pulled him closer still. He slithered up to the waiting beast. Whatever or whoever it was certainly must have seen him by now and was probably waiting for the perfect moment to make a move.

Uncle Fred stepped into the shadow of the dark creature looming above him. However, to his relief, the closer he got, the more obvious it became that this was no animal or any sort of monster at all. His heart slowed to a normal pace, and he began to carefully examine this strange thing, never once thinking about running inside. After a complete inspection, he recognized what he was looking at. It was, in fact, a cat tree almost like the one he played on at home. However, this cat tree was not as fancy as the one he had. Instead, it was a series of cardboard boxes, some ripped, some smelly with tomato stains. Each box had different colored carpet scraps glued unevenly on all sides. The boxes were somehow connected with thick glue and stacked one on top the other at a slight tilt. The entire cat tree teetered on what seemed to be a wide scooter. To Uncle Fred it looked fun and inviting, a playground just for him. He wanted to climb to the top and rest there until the end of his shift. Like a good guard, he would resist that temptation.

Uncle Fred ran his paw over the orange carpet strip and onto one of a musty, green ones. It tickled his paw. On the backside of the cat tree, he found a crumpled piece of paper stuck to the carpet with chewed caramel candy. Written on the paper was the word: *Stix* Now pretending he was a secret agent, Uncle Fred quickly surveyed the area. When he saw no one, he carefully removed the strange paper and unfolded it. It was definitely a letter written by someone with no more phonetic ability than him. He took the note in his paw, sat down, squinted his eyes and read:

Deer All stix

WE lop yu injoy this skraching Post.

PlEES EXCEPt this gift
or beHaFF ov all alley
WE r sorri For thE trvbEL
WE hav kavsED.
PlEEs taYk owr PEES
oFFFEr and
LEtz bE frEnds.

SinEd,

FidEL,

lEEdr ov allEYz.

"How wonderful!" Uncle Fred shouted with
delight. "The Alleys want to be our friends after
all!" He was about to run inside and read the note
to everyone, when a more interesting plan came to
mind. "I know," he beamed. "I'll sneak this cat tree
gift through the back and surprise the whole bunch.
They'll be so proud of me when they see what I have
done. Then everybody will play on the tree thanks to
me, and we can finally be friends with all the Alleys!"

Uncle Fred decided to drag the gift in through
the nearby loading dock. It was used in the old days to

Chapter Nine

Life Two

load and unload heavy crates or other large equipment for Mr. Stockwell and his umbrella business. Now, it remained locked and unused. Uncle Fred knew how to open it because as the guard of that area, he spent many boring nights playing with the lock just in case he needed a quick hideout or a quick route into the Factory.

With all his efforts, he heaved and moved the cat tree up to the loading dock, his noxious body sweat wreaking of old milk. "Boy, this thing is sure heavy," he said to himself. Still pretending he was a private eye, he moved the tree as if someone was after him, ducking and hiding around the sides, laughing at his own amusement. Finally, he opened the loading lock with his sharp claw and began to lower the huge, metal door. It formed a large ledge for lifting. The entire platform could be raised and lowered with a pulley. Suddenly, Uncle Fred sneezed, and the door fell with a crash to the concrete floor, sending a wave of dust in all directions. He coughed violently and whipped his tail out from under the powerful door. It throbbed something awful. Uncle Fred regained his composure and slid the cat tree onto the ledge. With all his newfound strength, acquired in Waffles' Workout, no doubt, he raised the ledge with the pulley, tugging until his paws burned. He knew Waffles would be particularly proud of him.

With one final surge Uncle Fred pushed the cat tree inside and slammed the door shut. The room around him was dark and dismal. All sounds echoed and bounced off the four, faraway, cracking walls. Uncle Fred happily moved the tree into the center of the deserted room and positioned it under a beam of moonlight creeping in through a gash in the ceiling wood. He took one last gleeful look at his accomplishment and ran to the others, the note dangling from his mouth.

Uncle Fred darted around until he found the rec room and waited outside while Mr. Sox spoke at his meeting.

"And so," Mr. Sox said, "the Alleys must learn that we are not beneath them. We are, in fact, superior to them. We will not accept Fidel as our leader, for he is our worst enemy. Yes, friends, the Alleys must learn their lesson!"

As Uncle Fred listened to Mr. Sox, he laughed to himself. Wouldn't Mr. Sox feel stupid for saying all those silly things? After all, Uncle Fred was the only Stick who knew the truth about how the Alleys really felt. They, too, wanted to be friends. Good friends. All this combat nonsense would finally soon be over.

"Mr. Sox! Mr. Sox!" Uncle Fred exploded after listening to enough babble.

Mr. Sox eyed him from the podium and continued speaking, "As I was saying, we Sticks have to--."

Uncle Fred came storming up to the podium and jumped on top of the green crate. "Stop, Mr. Sox!

Life Two

Stop speaking!"

"Uncle Fred!" Mr. Sox rebuked. "What is the meaning of all this? Can't you see we are having a meeting?" He waved his paws wildly for Uncle Fred to step down.

Uncle Fred looked out at his peers. They were all sitting on the floor staring up at him in disbelief. "But, Mr. Sox..." he mumbled.

"Hey!" Fluffy yelled from his pillow. "Aren't you a guard? Go back outside! What if something happens out there?"

"That's just it! Nothing will! Nothing will go wrong ever again!" Uncle Fred said excitedly.

Mr. Sox looked at him and stepped closer. "What are you talking about, son?"

"Get a load of this!" Uncle Fred slapped the note in front of Mr. Sox, and then stood proud grinning from ear to ear.

"What is it, Mr. Sox?" Romeo asked.

"Yeah? What is it?" others called from the back of the room.

Mr. Sox glared at Uncle Fred then carefully opened the note. He slid his wire-rimmed glasses up his nose and squinted. As he read, his expression changed. He suddenly looked stunned and bewildered. His bottom jaw dropped low, and his tail sunk to the ground.

"See, Mr. Sox? I told you everything had changed," Uncle Fred boasted.

Chapter Nine

Mr. Sox shook the podium violently. "Where is it?" he said with urgency. "Where is this *thing*? Don't tell me you--."

Uncle Fred smiled and nodded his head triumphantly.

"Oh no, Uncle Fred! Have you gone mad? Take me to the gift! *Now!*" Mr. Sox demanded.

Uncle Fred jumped off the crate quickly. Surely Mr. Sox misunderstood the letter. Still, he raced his mentor over to the gift. The others followed excitedly.

Everyone ran through the Factory to the abandoned room at the back. "Here it is!" he announced in the dusty doorway. "See? Isn't it beautiful?"

"How'd you get that in here?" Mr. Sox mumbled.

"I lifted it up on the loading dock," Uncle Fred explained, turning his nose to the others. "Who's the smart one now?"

"Stand back!" Mr. Sox shouted. "Nobody take a step!" He inched his way closer into the endless room. It was dark and full of dust. A roof of spider webs loomed above as his tiny footsteps echoed through the empty space. Everyone watched as Mr. Sox disappeared into the darkness. From the doorway, they were able to see the shape of the gift, though nobody could tell what it was. It stood there, tall and ominous, specks of moonlight bouncing around its top.

"Dude, it looks like a huge pile of mud," Twinkle Toes said.

Life Two

"Shhhh," Romeo whispered. "It doesn't look anything like mud."

Little by little they inched their way deeper into the room. Mr. Sox was nowhere in sight, and his footsteps no longer echoed through everyone's ears. Suddenly, Mr. Sox erupted from the darkness like a volcano. "Run! Run for your lives!" he wailed. "Hurry! There's no time to lose!" Mr. Sox's old body stormed out of the room when suddenly a low rumble, like a far away train, began to shake the floor. It quickly grew stronger and stronger. The rest of the Sticks stood paralyzed with fear, fur bloomed, backs arched, paws clenched.

"What is that?" Romeo yelled.

The rumble grew louder and more intense, until suddenly, a dreadful crackling filtered from the center of the room. Bizarre banging and ripping noises filled the air sending nasty chills up the Sticks' spines. They took a collective breath and for a brief moment there was an eerie wink of silence. Then, like a nightmare, a loud, thunderous explosion roared through the room. In a flash, dozens of angry Alleys burst out of the cat tree and zoomed through the Factory like a swarm of killer bees. With high-pitched, devilish laughs, they bulldozed the Sticks out of their way and went on a maniacal rampage destroying everything in sight. Mr. Sox's voice still screamed in the background. "Run, my children! Run for your lives!"

The Alleys charged through every room in

the Factory, knocking down tables, books, tools, paintings, you name it. They smashed the walls, scratched the floors, and savagely ripped the filling out of the pillows, stuffing it into a few Sticks' mouths. They found the soup pot and cut the rope with their sharp teeth, then turned it upside down and pounced, making a few big dents. In the library a few spiteful Alleys viciously tore apart the sacred books, littering the floor with torn pages and scraps of great literature. Others found the Stick School classroom and took evil pleasure in relieving themselves on the students' work, their crayons and yarn.

In a panic the Sticks raced toward the doors. Despite their intense combat training and supply of rubber band weapons, nobody expected anything like this. They weren't ready yet. To their shock the nasty Alleys were blocking all the entrances. They were now hostages inside their own safe harbor. The petrified Sticks watched as their beautiful palace quickly fell to the rotten paws of the Alleys. It was the ultimate Stick nightmare unfolding right before their eyes. Even Octavian watched nervously from the rafters.

Then out of the dusty, swirling cloud at the center of the rec room, the demon Fidel emerged. His eyes burned like two balls of fire, his teeth jutting out like knives. He growled deeply as his chest heaved violently up and down. Thick gobs of drool oozed from his mouth hitting the floor like water balloons. At that moment all the Sticks, even the Alleys, stopped

Life Two

moving. The room fell into a deadly silence as a diploma floated off the wall. Fidel stepped on it as he slowly patrolled the room eyeing everyone in his evil path. His joyful sneer was just as sickening to look at as his stench was to smell. Suddenly he leapt forward and snarled, "Where's Romeo?" Nobody moved. "I said, where's Romeo?"

"I don't see him, boss," Bait's voice echoed from under a pile of bent musical instruments that wound around his body like snakes. "He ain't here."

"Then just get somebody! We'll get Romeo next time!" Fidel thundered. "Sticks! Beware! This is only the beginning! Alleys, let's go!" With that, Fidel and the Alleys made one final, disastrous dash through the Factory, whizzing around like caged animals. Bait hobbled out with rusty instruments attached to his paws. When the dust finally cleared, there was no Alley to be seen.

Numbed by the invasion, the Sticks couldn't move. Making doubly certain the Alleys were gone, the Sticks slowly snapped out of their shock and looked around.

"Why?" Tabitha yelled. "Why?"

"I'll kill them myself!" Soot hollered.

Mr. Sox poked his head up from behind the broken podium and looked around the room, his gray ears still shaking. "Romeo? Somebody find Romeo!"

Everybody scrambled about calling out for him. Romeo was nowhere. Suddenly, Waffles zapped

Life Two

through Waldo's demolished photo lab and reached behind the smashed file cabinet. Finding the little blue door to the secret room, he opened it. To his surprise the scared Romeo was curled up into a tiny ball, shivering and trembling. "Oh, thank goodness!" Waffles cried. "Everybody, come quick! Romeo's all right!"

Romeo's eyes were sealed shut, and tears streamed down his furry face. His tail was tucked tightly under his belly. Mr. Sox knelt down to him and placed a friendly paw against his side. "It's okay, Romeo," he comforted. "They're gone now. You can come out."

Romeo, still quivering, looked up and cried, "Why me? Why does he want *me*?" He erupted into a million tears as Tabitha jumped to his side.

Mr. Sox just shook his head. He mumbled something to himself then announced, "Everybody, listen up. Make sure all of your friends are here. Every Stick must be accounted for." Everyone nodded their worried heads and grabbed tightly to their friends as they dashed out on one last search. Mr. Sox stayed with Romeo. They sat in silence for what seemed like an hour. "We were lucky this time," Mr. Sox assured Romeo. "Everyone is safe, I'm sure."

Suddenly, Fluffy came running into the tiny room panting and shaking. "Mr. Sox! Mr. Sox!" he screamed.

"Yes, Fluffy? What is it?"

Chapter Nine

"It's Twinkle Toes, sir," Fluffy wailed. "He's... he's gone!"

"Are you sure?" Romeo cried.

"Yes, Romeo, he's gone. We looked everywhere." Fluffy glared angrily at Uncle Fred who hadn't said one word this whole time.

Mr. Sox turned and numbly said, "It's the Alleys. They've got him."

Chapter Ten

Nobody went home for hours. The place was in shambles, disastrous and surreal. Everything they loved lay ruined on the ground. The clean up had already begun, as did the desperate search for Twinkle Toes. By the end of the night, Mr. Sox ordered everyone home. "We won't find him tonight," he announced. "There's no sense risking our own lives. We need to get a good night's rest and start fresh in the morning."

Little by little, the tired Sticks filtered out of the building knowing their lives had once again changed forever. They each took a long, mournful look at the rec room as they exited. Glancing around at the vandalized pillows and toys they so cherished, both sad and happy memories swelled in their heads. Of course, nothing was as bad as one of them being captured. It was all too much for the Sticks to bear, too much to correct in just one night. Mr. Sox was right; home was the best solution for the time being. The guards would stay during the night, shivering at their posts, while the others would rest before the long challenge of repairs that were needed began.

Uncle Fred was released from his shift indefinitely. Though his intentions were good, his mistake that night would forever dash any hope of him gaining the respect and admiration he craved. He sat alone in the corner of the rec room, sobbing under a pile of pillow feathers. Mr. Sox spotted him in his hiding place. "Go on home, Uncle Fred. There's nothing you can do tonight." Uncle Fred scrambled to get up, feathers stuck in his ears and nose. He faced Mr. Sox and took in a deep, bold breath. "M-Mr. Sox?" he whispered. "I-I-I'm, s-s-s-so sorry."

"I know," Mr. Sox said, staring into his teary eyes. "Just go home now and get some rest."

By ten o'clock everyone, even Mr. Sox, had left. Fluffy, Romeo, and Delio all walked home together per Mr. Sox's strict instructions. The streets were lonely and deserted. No one knew what to say to Romeo, so they walked in silence. He was once again the prime target of the entire event. At Romeo's building, Fluffy and Delio said their goodbyes and watched as Romeo slipped inside. Dennis was eagerly waiting for his cat.

"Where have you been?" Dennis asked from his bed. Relieved, he scooped up his Romeo and cradled

Life Two

him in his arms. Dennis opened his bedroom door and yelled to his mom. "He's home! Romeo's home!"

"All right," Mrs. Crumb called back. "Now get to sleep!"

Romeo felt safe in Dennis' room. Yet, tomorrow was still something to fear. The clean up would take forever and Combat School would most likely get more intense. As Romeo thought about the evening, he walked over to his chilly windowsill and pressed his nose against the cold glass. It began to drizzle and a slow wind swept through the city. Romeo's heart broke at the familiar scene across the alley, of Gwen clutching her dolls and crying. Surely, she worried why her new cat, Twinkle Toes, had not come home. Romeo wanted so badly to tell her that he'd find him. No matter what, he'd find him!

Later that same night Fidel and his entourage were busy boozing it up at Kitty's Cabaret. Claudia danced and tantalized her audience as Fidel, Bait, Cheeseburger, Stella, and Fidel's five cronies sipped their victory drinks at the front table. Stale dribbles of beer dripped down Fidel's chin and seeped into the holes of the bug jar, falling down like cannon balls on the helpless fireflies.

"Boy, Cheeseburger," Bait slurped, "you should've seen the look on dem Sticks' mugs! I never seen such scaredy cats before. Right Fidel?"

"Yeah," he mumbled. "Whatever." Fidel took a big gulp of beer and tossed Claudia a roach. She picked it up off the catwalk with her slinky tail and threw Fidel a wink. Stella folded her paws and lifted her nose to the air.

Cheeseburger wiggled his large, greasy body to face Bait. "I wish I could've been there tonight, but I guess I forgot. Sorry." He looked at Bait with a dumb, moronic expression.

Fidel rolled his eyes and snarled, "If you *ever* do that again, I swear, you'll be sorry!" He slammed his drink against the table, some of it splashing all the way up to Claudia. She slowly licked it off with her tongue. Stella turned away, quickly realizing her new boyfriend might not be Mr. Right after all. Still, she sat there just as the females before her. Cheeseburger coughed up a fur ball.

"Fidel?" Bait asked.

"Don't bother me during the show!" Fidel snapped.

"But boss," Bait pestered, "where's, you know, that Twinkle guy?"

Fidel growled at Bait, showing off his slimy, rotten jaws.

"Okay, okay," Bait stepped back. "I'll ask ya later."

Cheeseburger leaned into Bait and whispered, "I thinks he's with Max. I overheard Fidel saying they gots him locked in some box, and Max is watchin' him."

"Ooooo," Bait laughed ghoulishly.

 120

Life Two

"I said shut up!" Fidel hollered as he climbed onto the table. "This will teach you to listen to me!" He stomped around, kicking off the beer glasses and roaches to the floor. He concluded with a nasty hiss and calmly sat back down to watch the show. Claudia continued her dance nervously, stumbling around on the stage. Now and then, she leaned down getting deadly close to Fidel's face. He gave her a playful grin and threw her a kiss.

"Dats it!" Stella exploded. "Either she goes or I go!" Stella leapt onto the catwalk and knocked Claudia on her bottom. She grabbed her feather boa and wrapped it tightly around her neck. Claudia pulled it off, hissed, and managed to flip Stella onto her back. Claudia was now on top of her, ready to claw her to pieces. The crowd whistled and cheered, as did everyone at the front table. For the first time all night, Fidel seemed pleased. He loved a good catfight.

"Bait!" he called. "Get over here!"

"Yeah, boss?"

"Bait, don't forget the plan for tomorrow. Come find me as soon as it's complete," he scolded, keeping his devilish eyes focused on the stage. "And make sure Romeo is there. Now, get outta here."

"But...boss?"

"I said, get out! I don't wanna see you until tomorrow!" Fidel demanded.

"All right, all right, I get da point. I know when I'm not wanted." Bait slithered away from his chair

Chapter Ten

and zoomed out of the bar. The rest of the Alleys stayed to watch the exciting catfight escalate on the stage above.

The next day most of the Sticks arrived at the Factory much earlier than usual. Some had started cleaning up, while others helped guard the building. The night guards, who had watched the Factory with extra stress and caution, were awfully tired. Mr. Sox surveyed the entire structure for damage and estimated a one month reconstruction period. Not only was the place a mess, but several things, like the soup pot and library shelves, had to be rebuilt. As Romeo predicted, Mr. Sox was already planning on extra combat classes and less free time. It was quickly becoming clear that their lives were getting more difficult.

The primary focus for the day was to find Twinkle Toes. No Stick would rest until he had returned safely and unharmed. Mr. Sox was desperate for a plan.

Unbeknownst to the Sticks, Bait had slithered his way into the Factory through a small, hidden hole in the wall he had found some time ago. "What a dump!" he chuckled to himself.

Bait completed his one and only task in just minutes. He quickly crept out of the Factory and ran off to find Fidel, who he knew would be at the site of a brand new Alley club. It was set to open soon.

Life Two

The new hot spot promised nightclub atmosphere with plenty to eat and plenty to drink, as well as top of the line entertainment. It was a big deal to bored, excitement-starved Alleys in need of a new getaway. Max originally found the large space through a wide, rusted pipe beneath a human nightclub. The human club above supplied a built-in sound system as a result of the music that filtered through the walls. Max hired a crew to paint the place a deep purple and even managed to get his claws on some sparkly streamers, which he dangled from the ceiling. The entrance to the pipe was lined with bright red soup can labels and topped by a metal sign adorned with the name of the club. Max called it *The Glitterbox* and was currently auditioning dancers. Fidel came to watch.

"Excellent, excellent my dear...Priscilla," Max said, charming the young female on stage. "We'll be in touch."

Priscilla picked up her pretty props and smiled. "Thank you, thank you, Mr. Max." She tiptoed out of the club as the next wannabe entered.

In sauntered a curvy female with a shiny, black coat and painted claws.

"Raven?" Fidel hollered. "What are *you* doing here? I thought I told you to stay away." He looked her up and down and rubbed his scratchy chin.

"I'm auditioning for Max," Raven boasted with newfound confidence. "I'm sure that's all right with you, right, honey pie?"

Flustered, Fidel answered. "Do whatever you want. I don't care."

Raven gave Fidel a wicked wink and began her number. In her paw was a single rose, which she used as a microphone. She stood on the small stage, stared Max deeply in the eyes, and sang her heart out. Raven had a hypnotic, deep voice, which entranced any male Alley around. She sang "My Darling Clementine" with such passion, it almost seemed like it was her own life story. Fidel drooled on her every note, mesmerized by her talent. She sauntered about the stage, never seeming nervous or self-conscious, a major change since their last encounter. When she finished, she playfully threw the rose at Max and drifted off the stage. Max erupted into applause, as did Fidel. "You're hired!" Max called to her. "Be here tomorrow at eight for rehearsals."

Raven nodded with a sneaky smile and blew a kiss in Fidel's direction. "Wait, wait, Raven!" Fidel blundered. "Uh, why don't you meet me at Smelly's in say, one hour?"

"Of course," Raven answered with a gleam in her eye.

Both Alleys watched as her bottom swished and swayed itself into the pipe. "What a gal!" Max said.

"Uh, she's all right," Fidel said modestly. "If you like that type."

Life Two

Just then, Fidel noticed Bait lurking at the back of the room. He was hidden by a wall of silver tinsel, crouching behind an old shoebox.

"Bait!" Fidel snapped. "What are you doing back there? Did you finish your job?" Fidel's eyes turned red and glared at Bait.

Bait clawed himself out of the tinsel and stepped into the light. "Yeah, boss, it's all done. They didn't see me, not even my tail."

"Good, good," Fidel said, sinking into his chair. "Now, all we can do is wait. Clank, Fink, and Mustard should be arriving shortly, and as long as they finished *their* job, we should be well on our way to victory!"

"Yeah!" Max and Bait shouted.

"Shut up, you idiots!" Fidel yelled. "Now, I've got to go. I have a meeting with Claudia, and then I have to go to Smelly's to see Raven. Let me know if anything changes. No surprises, see?"

"Got it," Bait said.

Back at the Factory, Maybelle was snooping around the back rooms looking for some rags to mop up the gooey layer of Alley drool splattered around the floors. She found two rags, but also came across a strange paper with the word *Stix* on it. Spooked, she decided take it to Mr. Sox right away. She ran to the rec room as fast as she could.

"It was just sitting there on a broken typewriter,"

Chapter Ten

Maybelle explained. "I didn't know what to do with it, so I brought it to you."

"You did the right thing," Mr. Sox praised. "Now, let's see what we've got here." He gracefully put on his glasses and sat down on a pile of feathers. Other nearby Sticks gathered around as well. Carefully opening the paper, Mr. Sox quietly read the letter to himself. "Oh my goodness," he gasped. "I…I can't believe this! I just can't…!" He dropped it on the floor and ran out of the room. Romeo picked up the paper. It shook in his paws. With worried eyes, he read the letter to the others.

Stix,

IF yoo want yor preshvs
Twinkl Tose back then
yoo hav too get him tomoro at
thv gratE sta tw. He will bEE thar
at thv top wayting For yv. BE
on thv 5 o'clok pM Farry.
Must sEnt
    Misstr Shado
        Fliffy

Life Two

that FEMaiL with thv
    lonq lashES
thv ac ter
Thv too biq qvyz
    RoMEo!

SiNED,
  FiDEL,
lEEdr ov allEYz

Romeo crumpled up the paper in his paw and went to find Mr. Sox.

"What are we going to do?" he asked when he found him.

Mr. Sox took off his glasses revealing his weathered eyes. "There's only one thing for you to do. You have to find Twinkle Toes. There's a chance he's at the great statue just like Fidel said. Tomorrow at five o'clock you'll all be on that ferryboat! Now, run and tell the others. Then go home and get a good night's rest."

Later that night Romeo, Fluffy, Shadow, Tabitha, Calvin, Waffles, and Vittles nervously tossed and turned in their cat beds. None of them were able to sleep. Dozens of questions circled around in of their minds. Why did Fidel take Twinkle Toes to the

Chapter Ten

great statue? Why did he choose *only certain* Sticks to get him? Was this a trick? Maybe Fidel was going to be at the top of the statue ready to bludgeon them to pulp! Nobody could guess what was in his evil mind, but they knew they could never live with themselves if something happened to Twinkle Toes. After all the torture Twinkle Toes had been through, and to have finally found happiness, Romeo couldn't turn his back now. If Twinkle Toes was really there, he knew they'd find him. Rain or shine, they'd all be on that ferry.

Chapter Eleven

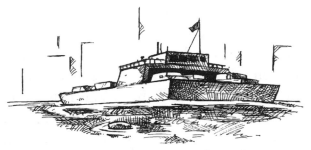

The next day Romeo and the others prepared themselves for their long journey to the city dock. Thousands of tourists flocked there every year to board the ferry that would take them to the most famous statue in the world. Her massive body stood proudly on her own private island. Waving to all the visitors, she blended into the thick, gray clouds that rested against the horizon. A gift from another land, her Highness represented hope and prosperity, pride and belief. Like a skyscraper, the majestic statue loomed above the polluted waters, calling to her fans. After their long and tiring walk, Romeo and his friends stood at the dock eyeing the statue in the distance.

"She's a beaut, ain't she?" Waffles cried.

"I wonder if Twinkle is really up there," Fluffy questioned as his eyes elevatored to the tippy-top of the statue. Dangling from Fluffy's ears were two glittery, clip-on earrings his person had put on him that morning. No one even commented. They were all quite used to his outrageous adornments. Fluffy twiddled the earrings with his paw.

Romeo stepped forward to the edge of the dock. "Well guys, let's go find Twinkle."

The seven Sticks carefully snuck onto the small, wooden ferry. Strangely, there were no camera-toting mobs of tourists as was the usual scenario. Aside from the ferry driver and the ticket seller, the dock was deserted. A short man inside the ticket booth announced the final boarding. "Everybody on!" he called to no one. "Aw, what's the point? Nobody's here anyway. All right, Finny," he said to the boat driver, "you should have about twenty people to pick up from the island. Hurry back so we can go to Mack's. He's holdin' the pool table for us."

"I'll be back soon as I can," Finny yelled from his perch behind the boat wheel.

Within minutes, they drifted away from the dock and headed out into the deep, blue ocean. The seven cats moved from their secret hiding spot and luxuriously sat on deck as if they actually belonged there. All fourteen eyes excitedly watched their city slip farther and farther away as they rocked to the beat of the wild waves. The water was choppy and rough, flinging the boat this way and that. Tabitha couldn't handle it. She flung her head over the side and vomited out every fly and fur ball she had inside her.

"Disgusting, absolutely disgusting!" Calvin snapped.

Tabitha looked at him with bloodshot eyes. "Well excuse me for having a sensitive stomach. What do you want me to do? Throw up on *you*?"

"Yuck. You are a foul creature, Tabitha," Calvin said, walking away.

Tabitha rolled her eyes and bit her blue lip. Once again, she felt the sharp pinch in her belly and fed the fish some more gruel.

From the deck, Romeo stood tall and proud in the wind as he watched the great statue come closer into view. "We're almost there!" he cried.

"Now remember, Romeo, this is not a vacation," Mr. Shadow instructed. "We have a job to do." He turned and faced the others. "Listen up everyone. Mr. Sox put *me* in charge, so when we get off this ship you must all listen to *me* and do as I say. As *I say*! Is that understood?" All six Sticks shook their furry heads, even Waffles and Vittles who were far too nervous and scared to be in control. They were all grateful to have an assigned leader.

The ferry ride lasted only twenty minutes. It docked at the far end of the island beside a small wooden ramp. There, a handful of tourists were eagerly waiting to leave. One by one, they jumped on the ferry with their souvenirs and screaming children. As they

Chapter Eleven

shuffled around for a seat, the seven cats secretly slipped off the boat and crawled onto a plank under the dock.

"Shhhh," Mr. Shadow whispered. "We'll get up as soon as the ferry leaves."

Everybody sat quietly and listened to the sound of crashing waters beneath their paws. The violent thrashing scared them as they waited for a safe moment to emerge. Quite delectably, a school of fish drifted by tempting Calvin.

"I'm hungry," he said licking his lips. "When do we eat?"

Vittles turned to him and snapped, "Go ahead, Mr. Bigshot. You jump right into the water and get yourself some fish."

"No thanks," Calvin said sarcastically.

"How could you be hungry at a time like this?" Mr. Shadow scowled. "Let's just find Twinkle Toes and get out of here!"

Soon the ferryboat puttered on its way back to the city. The Sticks crept up over the dock and took a quick look around. The island seemed deserted and creepy. It was very tiny, about three city blocks long from end to end. To the left was an ugly, yellow building with all kinds of touristy words on it like: *souvenirs*, *drinks*, and *restrooms*. The rest of the land was covered in muddy, patchy grass and a few stone benches facing the water. At the center of it all was the great statue herself. She stood magnificently, umpteen stories high on a large stone platform, grinning at her city in the distance. In her hand appeared to be a book and some sort of beacon light. The chiseled woman wore a drabby, stone gown and was a dull blue color from head to toe. All the Sticks tilted their heads as far back as they could to take in the awesome sight of this lady. Despite the recent bad things in their lives, this moment was masterful. Just the sight of her brilliance was like looking into another world, a grand, exciting world of dreams and fantasy.

"It's just a big, old rock," Calvin blurted out, breaking the silence. "I think I can see up her skirt."

"Awe, shut up, will you?" Mr. Shadow cracked. "Why must you always be such a cynic, Calvin? This is a once in a lifetime opportunity for us. Come on, everybody. We've got a job to do."

Everyone marched single file up to the statue's feet. They played around for a bit on her toe nails and shoe straps. Mr. Shadow had to be pried out from between two of her toes after he slipped and got his paw caught between them. He dusted himself off and ordered everyone into the hollow center of the statue. There, a long staircase zigzagged all the way to the top, but a more useful route was a nearby elevator. "It's like the one in my building," Romeo exclaimed. "I even know how to use it."

"*Everyone* knows how to use an elevator," Calvin said rudely.

"Oh, lay off," Tabitha moaned. "I wish you

Chapter Eleven

hadn't come with us, Calvin."

"Now, now," Mr. Shadow interrupted. "Either we all get along or we just go home, and that won't do anybody a bit of good."

"Sorry," Calvin and Tabitha said in unison.

"That's a lot of stairs," Romeo remarked eyeing the miles and miles of steps. He jumped up high enough to press the call button for the elevator. Soon, something clicked, and the two huge, metal elevator doors opened revealing a yucky mess of candy wrappers and melted popsicles.

"And they complain about us," Waffles chuckled to himself.

They all quickly stepped inside. Fluffy pressed another button sending everyone soaring up to the top. Higher and higher they rose. Tabitha felt the familiar rumble in her tummy and began to burp and gag.

"Not here, Tabitha," Mr. Shadow pleaded. "Wait until we get off."

"I'll try," Tabitha struggled, clutching her stomach.

To most of the Sticks, this was a very exciting moment. The speed of the elevator rattled their bodies around like a carnival ride. Sure, they were scared too. They didn't know what would happen once the elevator doors opened. Would Fidel be there with his needle sharp claws? Would Twinkle Toes be alive? Would a human greet them? The mystery of it all excited the cats and lured them further into this world of adventure.

Life Two

When the elevator finally stopped, all eyes went to Mr. Shadow. Nobody moved. They had reached the top, hanging in the elevator for what seemed like hours. Then, the doors opened sending a whipping wind passed them. Mr. Shadow, being the official leader, was the first to exit. Nervously, he marched out the doors one paw at a time and disappeared around the corner. "It's all right," he called back. "You can come out now."

Slowly, the others followed. There was no Fidel and no people, but unfortunately there was no Twinkle Toes either. There was, however, a most magnificent view of the city and beyond. When Romeo looked off into the distance, he could see all the marvelous buildings he was so familiar with. They looked like toy blocks against the patchy, gray sky. Farther still beyond the city, Romeo could make out a cluster of more tiny buildings. He wondered if that place was like his city, filled with rotten alley cats and grisly dogs. Or was it a pleasant place with happy people and warm, sunny days? From the summit where he stood, everything looked peaceful and calm, quite a difference from being up close. Dizzying thoughts filled his mind as he caught a glimpse of City Park, instantly remembering that fateful day. Without warning, Mr. Shadow broke his concentration.

"Oh no!" Mr. Shadow screamed.

"What is it? What's wrong?" Romeo hollered.

Mr. Shadow stepped forward above the statue's

Chapter Eleven

left ear and said, "Look! There's another note. I found
another darn note." He read it to the group.

Stix

Got yv Agen!!!
Yv won't fynd yor frend
Here!
In Fakt, yoo wont' fynd him
at all. HE iz not here and
Yor not goEng any wer.
Look intoo thv watr at
thv botE sayling away.
Didnt' yvv no thv sailerz were
on stryk? Yor botE waz thv
last botE for a vary
long tyme. hav Fvn Et
yor new Home.
Sined,
Fidel,
Leedr ov alleyz.
.PS. iyl tayk goood care
vv thv Faktori.

Chapter Eleven

"What does it all mean?" Tabitha blundered.

"He's right! Fidel is right!" Waffles said as he fidgeted around trying not to be an alarmist. "How could I forget! All sailors went on strike! Even the ferry drivers are on strike! That boat must be the last one of all! There won't be another one until the strike is settled! We're stranded here! Damn that Fidel! He tricked us! We'll never get home now!"

"Wait just a darn minute, Waffles!" Mr. Shadow responded. "You mean to tell me you knew there wasn't another boat coming back and didn't say anything? Now we're stuck on this island until the strike is over! That could be weeks! Months!"

"Get me out of here!" Fluffy whined in a growing panic, flinging himself against the elevator doors. "Get me outta here now!"

Vittles bolted for the elevator, "I'm not staying on this island! See that boat out there?" He pointed to the last ferry that was half way back to the city. "If we swim fast enough we can catch it. Come on! Who's with me?"

"I am!" Waffles announced.

"I can't swim!" Tabitha cried.

"You can do it!" Waffles yelled. "All your endurance training is about to pay off! You're stronger than you realize!"

"But...but...," Mr. Shadow stuttered. He was the leader, but seemed to have no good suggestions for anyone.

Life Two

Waffles and Vittles dove into the elevator and pressed the down button. Everyone jumped in after them and squeezed themselves to the walls. Mr. Shadow was scared, but he didn't let on. He had to be strong for the others.

The elevator reached the bottom, and the doors opened. They all stormed out, following Waffles and Vittles in a mad dash for the dock. The ferry was already far away. "Let's go!" Waffles hollered. "We can do it!"

Vittles jumped into the cold water first, his brother Waffles followed. Being experienced swimmers, they were confident in their abilities. As their bodies splashed in, they disappeared beneath the surface for several seconds. When they bobbed back up, their teeth were chattering, and their noses were blue. They treaded the water hard. "Hurry! The longer we wait, the more we'll have to swim, see?" Vittles shouted.

From the very edge of the dock, Romeo and the others stared at the blurry water below. They couldn't move. They couldn't jump. They just stood like lumps of clay. Calvin had a very important audition the next day for a pet shaving cream ad. Motivated by another chance at fame, he yelled, "I'm going! I can't stay here! I just can't! I've got to get to that audition! It could be my big break!" He closed his eyes, held his breath, and counted to three. "One..two..two and a half..three!" With his back paws he leapt off the wooden platform and did a perfectly painful belly flop into the water. His

Chapter Eleven

body hit hard making an awful sound. He screamed and wailed and gasped for air, but he made it.

"Are the rest of you coming or not?" Vittles screamed as he bobbed in the ocean, his words bubbling. "We've got to swim now!"

The remaining cats looked at Mr. Shadow for guidance, but he seemed as frightened as anyone. "I... I...can't!" he blurted. "I just can't jump! I'm...afraid of the water!"

"Me too!" Tabitha yelled.

It was painfully obvious. They weren't going anywhere. Waffles and Vittles looked up with their red, salty eyes and blinked goodbye. Their little paws paddled faster and faster toward the ferryboat as their mouths sucked in gobs of dirty water. Calvin pushed and pushed, though the current was too much for him. He fought to keep his head above water, but he kept going under.

"Keep breathing!" Waffles screamed. "Just don't sink!"

Still, Calvin trailed far behind. "Stop!" he choked. "Help!" His little body couldn't keep up. Exhausted, he stopped paddling, bobbed in the water and wept. Beneath him, his back paws still peddled like crazy trying to keep him afloat. By now, Waffles and Vittles were nearly out of his sight and sure to reach the ferry. Calvin tried to swim once more, but he had no strength left. His strength finally gave out, and he slowly began to slip beneath the surface. The others watched in horror from the deck.

"Swim! Come back!" Romeo shouted. "You can do it, Calvin! Come back to us!"

"Swim, Calvin!" Fluffy urged. "Swim for your life!"

But, it was no use. Calvin was going nowhere but down.

"We've got to do something!" Tabitha cried quickly. "He needs help!"

Without thinking, Fluffy dove into the water and swam with all his might. He pushed and paddled and grunted toward Calvin. The others watched and prayed. Coming up for air, Fluffy could see Calvin sinking lower and lower until only the tips of his two orange ears stuck out like upside-down goldfish.

Calvin took one last gasp and went under, slipping into unconsciousness. Reaching him just in the nick of time, Fluffy opened his mouth as wide as he could and bit into Calvin's neck just before he plunged deeper into the water. He pulled with every bit of energy he had left. Fluffy dragged Calvin's limp body through the water toward the island. When they reached the dock, Fluffy could barely breathe. "Here…" he huffed heavily to the others. "Take…him…first."

Romeo and Mr. Shadow reached into the water and heaved Calvin onto the dock. Then they did the same for Fluffy, who collapsed from exhaustion onto the ground. The two soggy cats lay like two dead fish waiting to be scaled. Bits of water spouted from their

Chapter Eleven

mouths. Suddenly, Calvin began to cough his way back into consciousness, and Fluffy, overcome by the whole situation, started to sob out of relief. He never noticed that his clip-on earrings drowned in the rescue.

"That was amazing, Fluffy," Tabitha sighed, trying to comfort him. "I've never seen anything like it. You were so brave."

Fluffy lifted his head long enough to see that Calvin was safe and in good paws.

As the two drenched cats rested, Romeo could see the ferryboat almost reaching the harbor, and two little dots on deck. *They made it,* he thought to himself. *Those lucky bums made it.* Maybe he should have tried to swim for it too. After all, he was much stronger than he used to be. He resolutely walked over to the others and sat down. "Well, now what do we do?"

They were stranded, and they knew it. It was time to face facts. "We need a plan," Mr. Shadow said. All tired eyes turned to him. He cleared his throat and calmly continued. "We need a plan to get out of here."

"Plan? Of course we need a plan!" Romeo snapped.

"What kind of plan?" Tabitha whined.

Mr. Shadow looked up into the deep sky. "I don't know, Tabitha. I just don't know, but if we put our heads together surely we'll come up with something."

"Well," Romeo said. "What would *Mr. Sox*

do right now? He always has a good answer for everything."

"He'd probably kill us for not jumping in the water, that's what he'd do," Fluffy coughed, shaking his fur dry.

"No way," Romeo disagreed. "He'd be proud that we didn't try. There's no way we all would have made it to that boat."

"But *they* made it!" Tabitha snapped.

"Yes," Mr. Shadow replied. "Because they're fitness cats, stronger than most. And I bet even *they* struggled. Besides, when they get back into the city, I just know they'll send help for us. You'll see." He sat down and chewed his claws frantically. "The best thing we can do is wait."

Fluffy rolled over, spit out some water and said, "Something must be terribly wrong in the city. I mean, think about it. What awful thing is Fidel up to that he sent us all out here? What's he going to do? Oh gosh, I hope he's not hurting anyone!"

"You're scaring me, Fluffy!" Tabitha screamed louder. "The world is ending!"

Mr. Shadow gathered everyone together. "Look, there's no sense in losing our minds," he reaffirmed. "Until help arrives, we are just going to have to survive here. It can't be too bad. After all, no Alleys are here. So, let's explore the island and set up camp. We will need places to sleep and food to eat."

"We're going to die!" Calvin blurted out,

wiggling in his wet spot. "We're going to starve to death! Our bodies are going to rot, and worms are going to eat our eyeballs!"

"Don't be ridiculous, Calvin," Mr. Shadow scolded. "Nobody's going to die!"

"Yes we are!" Tabitha wailed.

"Oh, no!" Calvin rang. "I think I'm starving to death already!"

"Stop it! Stop it right now!" Mr. Shadow demanded. "There will be no more of this insanity! It's not going to get us anywhere! *Anywhere!*" He rolled his eyes and scratched his head. "Now, I'm open to suggestions. Anything at all."

"Maybe we should divide up into groups," Romeo suggested.

"No, I don't want to!" Tabitha worried. "I'd feel safer if we were all together." She took a long look at the desolate island around her.

"All right then, it's settled. We stay together." Mr. Shadow guaranteed. "Besides, there's safety in numbers."

Everyone nodded in approval. Romeo and Tabitha helped Fluffy up, pulling off some seaweed that was stuck to his ear.

The group wandered around nervously. They trudged through the wet grass and patches of weeds. All the little luxuries they were used to, like cat food and cat litter, were obsolete. No people to play with here. No cozy laps to nuzzle in. Though no one dared mention it, there seemed to be no food at all. Not even a bird. Every-so-often they spotted a fly or some ants, but could they survive on insects alone? After all, they were domestic cats used to good food.

"We're going to die! We're going to die! We're going to die!" Calvin mumbled over and over, his head to the ground. Fluffy smacked him in the shoulder and told him to shut up for the hundredth time, but Calvin was already coming unglued.

As they walked in silence, Romeo heard Tabitha sniffling from the back of the line. He let her catch up to him. "Tabitha?" he called. "Why are you still crying?"

"I want to go home! I want to go home!" she cried, collapsing to the ground in tears, pounding on the dirt.

Mr. Shadow halted the group and rushed to her side. "Oh, no! Not again!" He sat beside her. "Look, Tabitha, I know how you feel. We all want to go home, and we all will go home soon. I promise. But, crying isn't going to help." He wiped the tears from her face. "You can do this, Tab. Think about what you learned in your survival classes. Fidel can't get rid of us this easy."

Tabitha looked up at him with her watery eyes. "It's not just me I'm worried about. I'm so worried about my person. She's been so careful with me since I went to the Pound. I don't want her to be upset."

Romeo knelt down next to her, "Well, she's going to be worried. All our people will. That's a given. But, just imagine how happy they'll be when we all--."

Just then, a noise caught Romeo's attention. He stopped talking and froze.

"When we all what, Romeo? What were you going to say?" Tabitha sniffed.

Romeo had a strange look on his face. "Shhh," he whispered, his eyes darting back and forth. "I think I heard something." He pointed to a cluster of nearby bushes. "Coming from over there."

"I knew it!" Calvin blurted. "It's all over! The aliens are attacking!" He ducked to the ground and flung mounds of dirt over his body.

"Hush up!" Fluffy snapped as quietly as he could. "Let's listen."

All ears tilted to the bushes. For a moment the only sound they heard was the lapping of the rough waters. Hardly aliens. But then, the eerie rustling got louder. This time everyone heard.

Mr. Shadow carefully leaned forward and whispered through his teeth, "Nobody move. It could be Fidel. Stay back, and be ready to strike." He took one tiny, cautious step, then another, and another in the direction of the bushes that were about ten feet away.

"Wait! Don't go!" Romeo mouthed under his breath, reaching for Mr. Shadow's tail. But it was no use. Mr. Shadow signaled for the others to stay back as he crept cautiously to the mass of bushes, never once looking back. Everyone did as he said, biting their claws nervously.

Mr. Shadow's heart pounded like never before. He was creeping closer and closer to the green bush, and farther and farther away from his friends. Suddenly, he heard the rustling again and flinched. Instinctively, he leapt back, falling on his butt. Bouncing up, he continued his prowl. Then, a most vile, angry hiss blared from the center of the bushes. The leaves rattled around wildly. Despite all his combat school teaching, Mr. Shadow let out a howl and darted away. He dashed away toward the base of the statue in a blazing trail of mud.

"Wait! Wait!" the others shouted, charging after him trying to catch up. Running faster than he ever thought possible, Mr. Shadow was already halfway up the long staircase.

Calvin looked back and saw something strange emerge from the bushes. "It just ran out of there!" he screamed. "It's coming this way! Faster, everyone! Faster!"

All the cats pumped harder up the steps. Almost to the top, Mr. Shadow's body collapsed. His legs burned, and he gasped for air. Fluffy pressured him to continue. They could all feel the vibrations of someone, or something, closing in on them. Romeo grabbed Mr. Shadow by the neck and tried to pull him the rest of the way. He couldn't do it. Just then, heavy, labored breathing filtered through the shaft, chilling everyone to the bone. They stood frozen solid in fear, all except for Calvin who raced up the stairs alone. Then, from nowhere, something lunged forward, hissing out of control.

"It's a monster! It's a monster!" Mr. Shadow howled, face to face with the hideous beast. He struggled to his feet as he reached for the next step. In Shadow's panic, his paw slipped, sending him crashing down the many stairs.

"Wait!" the beast hollered.

Mr. Shadow tumbled farther and farther. The noise was horrible. The other cats dashed down the stairs to save him. "Whoooo!" Mr. Shadow screamed, knocking his head on every step, having gained enough speed to launch a missile. Still five stories up, he punched through a window, shot out of the stair shaft, and landed outside on the statue's arm. His battered body slid down her long dress, toboggan style. He was then flung high into the air as if he had just been launched.

"Look! There he is!" Romeo shouted and pointed. They all watched stunned as their island leader plummeted toward the ground. He somersaulted in mid-air, coming dangerously close to a nearby flagpole. Lunging for the flag, he caught the bottom corner. Because of the wind, the flag angrily whipped and snapped and flung him into a tree. For a moment he disappeared in the mess of leaves and branches. Then, like a cannon, he shot out the bottom, bounced off a stone bench, landed in a big mud puddle and slid another ten feet, finally stopping right next to the bushes he originally ran from. It was the worst, most disastrous fall any of them had ever seen. The others rushed to his side, forgetting about the creature that had taunted them into this mess.

"Mr. Shadow! Mr. Shadow!" Tabitha roared as she ran up to him. "Are you all right? Are you alive?"

Mr. Shadow laid with his eyes closed tightly, his paws dangling in the mud. "Is he dead?" Romeo asked with great hesitation.

"I don't know," Fluffy said. "Who could survive a fall like that?"

Just then, Mr. Shadow tried to lift his head, moaning. It fell back down like a rock, and he immediately started to wheeze.

"Well, I guess that answers your question." Romeo smiled with relief. "Mr. Shadow is one tough cat!"

"Whoa," Tabitha sighed. "That was a close one."

Everyone was too distracted by Mr. Shadow and his clown-like fall to notice something lurking in the bushes again. Fluffy finally saw the branches move. "Calvin stop trying to scare us." Fluffy turned to the others. "I bet he's embarrassed that he ran away."

"Hey, guys," Calvin shouted, running toward them from the other direction, drenched in his own sweat. "Where'd that *thing* go? Did you kill it?" He took a long look at Mr. Shadow lying on the ground.

Chapter Eleven

"What happened to him?"

"Wait a minute!" Fluffy blurted, looking at the bushes, then back again. "If you're here, then who's-ahhh!"

Bam! The beast leapt from the bush. Everyone screamed in shock at the grotesque creature. It was a cat with pink fur on one side and no fur on the other. Its skin was a bright green color, and its right eye was black as coal. The left eye was missing, and an orange marble took its place. There was what seemed to be a human nose growing out of its back, one nostril pierced with a hook and a paper tag. One back leg was actually a manual can opener, the kind Mrs. Crumb used to open Romeo's cat food. Its tail had been split in two and curled up into little balls. The fur on its tummy hung to the floor in a matted mess. Both ears were turned inside out and twitched continuously. Finally, one small walrus tooth jetted from its mouth.

"It's an alien!" cried Calvin. "I told you! I told you! He's going to slice us to pieces with that leg!"

"No, wait!" the beast pleaded. "I'm not an alien! I'm a cat, like you. I'm not going to hurt anybody."

"You're a cat?" Romeo said with doubt as he squinted his eyes. "Man, what happened to you?"

"Why did you hiss at us if you're not going to hurt us?" Fluffy asked in his scariest karate pose.

"Because," the cat explained, "I thought you were Alleys, I hate Alleys. But now I can see that you're Sticks, just like me."

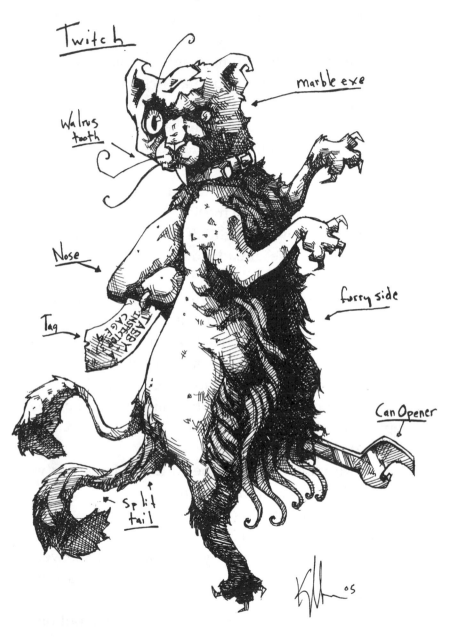

Life Two

Twitch

marble exe

Walrus tooth

Nose

Tag

furry side

Can Opener

split tail

Chapter Eleven

"You must think we're stupid," Calvin snapped.

"A Stick, huh?" Romeo said cautiously, looking the cat up and down. "You're a Stick? Where's your collar then?"

"I know it's hard to imagine, but I am."

"I believe him, guys. He's okay," Romeo said with trepidation.

"How do *you* know, Romeo?" Calvin argued. "He looks awful weird to me."

"I just know, all right? If he was going to hurt us, he would have already done so," Romeo said, hoping he was right.

The strange cat sat down on a rock and dropped his can opener leg in the mud. His ears started shaking back and forth, and his head bobbed around like a balloon. He sensed their curious eyes starring at him. "I've looked like this ever since...ever since..."

"You can tell us," Tabitha said, easing up. She kept a careful eye on Mr. Shadow. "What's your name? Where do you come from?"

"My name is Twitch," he huffed. "Maybe you've noticed I've got this nasty twitch."

Everyone did notice his peculiar way of twitching, almost like he'd been struck by lightening.

"No offense, but, why do you look like...well, like you do?" Fluffy asked with as little rudeness as he could possibly muster.

"Well," Twitch began, "it all started about one

year ago. Yes, one year to be exact. I was living with a painter named Stanley on the lower west side. We had a good life, good food, good times. He made a decent living and even talked about getting another cat for me to play with. I was looking forward to that," he added with a frown. "One day, when Stanley was off at a gallery trying to sell his work, I went outside for a walk. I met up with some friends, and we somehow got into a game of tug o' war over some stupid mouse. Well, you can already guess what happened next. The Alley cats came and started scratching us with their sharp claws. Two of my friends got away, but me and my girlfriend Cleo were tossed around like baseballs."

"Was it Fidel?" Romeo asked.

"No, I don't think so. Anyway, they were really rough just the same. So, we were getting pummeled, blood everywhere, the Alleys enjoying every minute of it. Next thing I know, they hit my head against a rock, and I passed out cold. I still don't know what happened to Cleo," he said with a tear. "When I woke up I found myself all alone in a cramped cage at the Pound. I was terrified. I sat there day after day waiting for Stanley, but he never came. After about a week, a scrawny old woman opened the cage door and dragged me into a truck with another cat named Steve. The truck driver took us to a laboratory where they do horrible things to animals." Twitch closed his eyes and twitched violently.

Just then, Mr. Shadow's eyes shot open. He

immediately saw the grotesque cat before him and went into a panic. "What's...what's going on here?" he demanded. "What is that thing? Kill it! Kill it!"

"Sit back, Mr. Shadow," Romeo insisted. "You're hurt. His name is Twitch."

"I am not hurt! I'm just fine, and I'm in charge here!" Mr. Shadow attempted to stand up but instantly fell down in torturous pain. It was obvious that his back legs were broken and his entire body badly bruised. "Oooohh!" he wailed.

"Stay still, Mr. Shadow," Fluffy said. "You're really hurt."

"Oh, no!" Tabitha cried. "What'll we do now? Mr. Shadow is our leader! How's he going to get us out of here?" Her eyes filled with tears.

"That's right," Romeo added. "Oh, this is terrible!"

"We're stuck here forever! Forever, I tell you!" Calvin yelled as loudly and as dramatically as he could.

"Calm down, children. Calm down. We can do this," Mr. Shadow said pointing to Twitch. "But who is this...thing? And what is he doing here? He could be a monster!" He threw his paws over his eyes like a child, his hind legs lifeless.

"No, no," Tabitha said between her sobs. "We've been through this. Really. He's a Stick, Mr. Shadow. He was telling us his horrible story."

Twitch twitched his entire body into a frenzy

while the others tried subtly not to watch, though they did anyway. "I was experimented on at a laboratory," he said to Mr. Shadow. "I know what it's like to be in great pain, just like you're feeling now."

Twitch could feel Mr. Shadow believed him. Calvin walked in circles around the entire group, slowly and creepily.

"They do these ghastly things," Twitch went on, getting dizzy from Calvin's paranoia, "for no earthly reason I'll ever understand. I used to be a cute, cuddly, white and brown cat. After six weeks of the most ungodly experiments, I not only look like the freak you see today, but I'm also a...a..."

"You're a what?" Romeo asked nervously.

"I'm a niner." He rolled over on his human nose and cried like a kitty, tears sprouting from his one remaining eye. "Yes, they did this to me. It was awful!" Everyone gasped.

Tabitha knelt next to him, "Does that...nose work?"

"Tabitha! That's not very nice. You shouldn't ask such things," Mr. Shadow groaned from the mud.

"It's all right, don't worry. I need to talk about it," Twitch sobbed, gaining control of his emotions. He rolled back onto his stomach and said, "One time, they woke me up real early. I had a tummy ache because of some foul meat they made me eat. Anyway, they took me out of my cage and put me on this really cold table. It was so shiny I could even see my face in it, only it looked all blurry and mangled. So, they wanted to see what would happen if they put potato salad in my eye. They took a big spoonful and shoved all the yucky mess under my eyelid. Man, did that hurt, especially the bits of onion. I squirmed around, but some lady held me down. She kept yelling at me to calm down, but who could calm down with potato salad in their eye?"

The rest of the cats shrugged their shoulders and looked at each other. "Why did they do that in the first place?" Tabitha asked, clutching her tail.

"Who knows?" Twitch continued. "I think it had something to do with the mayo company. I heard they had a problem with the mayonnaise causing weird side effects in children. Anyhow, that's how I lost my eye. They had to take it out with a spoon to scrape off all the potato salad. Pretty sick, huh?" His body twitched tossing him on his side. "And yes, the nose works."

"Ugh," Tabitha churned. "Sounds awful! Absolutely awful!"

"What does your tag say? The one on your *other* nose," Mr. Shadow inquired.

Twitch turned around and allowed everyone to get a good look at his human nose. "Well, first of all, don't even ask me about this experiment. It's just too darn gross to even get into. But, I don't know what the tag says. I can't read. Can you guys read?" he asked with a smile.

"Yes," Romeo blushed proudly. "We all can

Life Two

read. Every one of us." He stepped up to Twitch and carefully went for the tag. The closer Romeo got, the more Twitch's body shook. "It's all right, I'm not going to hurt you." Romeo reached out his paw and grabbed the tag. He didn't let on, but he was more than a little nauseous at the sight of a human nose protruding from a cat's backside. Romeo was sure the others felt the same way. In fact, Tabitha had to excuse herself two times to go purge in the bushes. She blamed it on seasickness, though they had been off the boat for quite some time. Fluffy leaned in closer inspecting not only the tag, but Twitch's entire laboratory-damaged body. Mr. Shadow still laid moaning and groaning from his catastrophic fall.

"Let me see," Romeo said. "It says: Tabby A. Inspector 37. Cage 9." Romeo stepped back and released the tag. "Hmm, nothing too exciting, I guess."

"I've always wondered about that thing," Twitch said. "I guess I always hoped there was some famous poem or saying on it, not just a bunch of numbers. Nobody likes to just be a number."

"Well, buddy," Fluffy smiled. "Not this time, but hey, it looks cool just the same."

"I guess so," Twitch said, though he looked sadly disappointed.

"Twitch?" Tabitha asked. "Do you know a way off this island? Please tell me you do. Tell me you can help us!"

"Well," Twitch rubbed his orange marble eye,

157

Chapter Eleven

"without the ferry boats, there isn't much that can be done. Sorry."

"And without Mr. Shadow...we're...doomed!" Calvin exploded.

"Hey, I may be hurt, but I'm not dead," Mr. Shadow moaned. "Now tell me, Twitch, do you have any friends here?"

Twitch shook his head.

"Are you alone on this island?" Mr. Shadow continued.

"Yeah," he answered with a frown. "It's just me here. I miss Cleo and my old friends. There used to be a mouse I played around with, but he's dead. I had to eat him."

"You sound pretty pathetic, if you ask me," Calvin snubbed. He was definitely not into this guy.

"Calvin!" Mr. Shadow snarled. "Why would you say such a thing? I liked you better a minute ago when you were scared of him."

"Whatever," Calvin muttered. He stared curiously at Twitch and kept his mouth shut.

"How did you get here?" Romeo asked, keeping a close eye on Calvin and his weird behavior. "I mean, if you were at that lab all that time, how did you end up here?"

They listened for Twitch's answer. It had been a question on everyone's mind, though they were too afraid to ask. Afraid of being impolite.

"Back at the lab," Twitch explained, "life was

really tough. I hardly got to eat, and I couldn't stand the experiments anymore. So, one day when they took me out of my cage, I took a chance and bit the doctor very hard. He jumped back and knocked over the nurse. As they fumbled around on the floor, I ran out the door and raced through the building. I had no idea where I was going or what I was doing. Finally, I saw a window in the kitchen. I leapt as high as I could over a guy eating green cereal and jumped out the window. They all came running after me. It was hard to run with a kitchen tool for a leg, but somehow I managed. My buddy didn't make it. He unfortunately had tin cans for legs. Anyway, the lab is right near the pier where the ferries dock. Behind me I could see all the doctors running after me, and I knew I had only two choices."

"What were they?" Fluffy asked on the edge of his seat.

"I could either let them catch me or jump on the ferry that was leaving. So, I jumped on the boat, and here I am. They did come to the island looking for me a few times, but I managed to hide. I'm a good hider." Twitch stood proud, grinning quivering ear to quivering ear.

Romeo looked confused. "Well," he pestered. "Why are you still here? Why didn't you take another ferry back?"

"What do you think would happen to a cat like me in the city? I mean, look at me. The Alleys would get me for sure!"

159

Chapter Eleven

"Nonsense," Mr. Shadow groaned from his comfy grass pile. "You're coming home with us! You have shown incredible courage and deserve to be rewarded. It would be a crime to spend your final life here alone. No, you will come back with us and live at the Factory. Everyone there will treat you like family, and that's final!"

Twitch was overcome by Mr. Shadow's generosity of spirit.

"If the Factory is still there when we get back," Calvin nudged to Fluffy. Fluffy bumped him back.

"Well," Twitch said uneasily. "We can talk about that later. Why don't I show you around the island, not that there's much to see. There are some spots, however, that you'll need to avoid."

A silence fell over the cats.

"I'm scared," Tabitha whined. "What about Mr. Shadow? We can't just leave him here! What if something happens? Something horrible?"

"I'll be all right for now," Mr. Shadow explained. "The mud I'm on is comfortable enough. Don't worry. Nobody's going to eat me, if that's what you're worried about, I think."

"Of course not, Mr. Shadow," Tabitha reassured. "I know. I'll stay with you. I can look around later. In fact, I'm going to gather some long weeds to wrap up those legs of yours. I need you feeling better as soon as possible."

Mr. Shadow patted her on the head and groaned.

Life Two

He was happy for the company. The others were on their way.

Calvin trailed behind in silence. "Uh, I'll be right back guys," he suddenly announced. "I forgot to tell Mr. Shadow something." Romeo, Fluffy, and Twitch continued on as Calvin ran back to the bushes. He bent down next to Mr. Shadow and whispered, "How do we know this Twitch guy is for real?"

"Just what do you mean, Calvin?" Mr. Shadow asked.

"Well, look at him! How do we really know he's not on Fidel's side? Maybe a spy! How can we trust a screwed up cat like that? Shouldn't we ask him more questions?"

"Calvin," Mr. Shadow responded. "I'm sure everything he said was true. Normally I'd be worried, but just look at him. Why would he lie? If he were going to hurt us, he would have done it by now. You're just being paranoid. You've got to snap out of it. You're driving everyone crazy! The poor guy's lonely. Now, why don't you go catch up with them and quit being so suspicious."

Calvin rubbed his chin. "I guess. But, I don't know, I mean, aside from the fact he's got a nose on his back and a funny leg and stupid ears, there's just something not right about him."

Calvin dashed off and caught up with the others near a garbage can full of food wrappers and other trash. Mr. Shadow scratched his muddy head.

Chapter Twelve

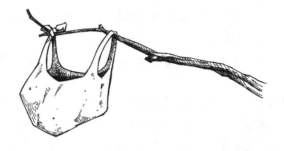

Tabitha scavenged around for some wooden sticks, big leaves, and any sort of string. She was simply desperate for a sure-fire remedy. Returning with two thick twigs, some newspaper, and an old shoelace that she bit in two, she had all the things needed to help Mr. Shadow. He lay on the ground miserable and still unable to move. His body ached something awful, and his broken legs throbbed and burned. "What's the newspaper for?" he asked.

She hastily unraveled the comics. One of them showed a cat getting eaten by a gorilla. "I'm going to wrap your legs in them, like casts. The leaves around here are far too small." She folded the newspaper into a perfect rectangle. "I've got to get this just right."

"You're not going to *touch* my legs! You hear me?" Mr. Shadow blurted pathetically.

Life Two

"Now, Mr. Shadow," she said motherly. "I've got to do it! You know very well your legs need to be cared for. Sorry, but you don't want them healing in that crooked position, do you?"

Mr. Shadow lifted up his head high enough to see his twisted, back legs. They were all scrunched up and deformed looking. They looked more like twigs than the actual ones Tabitha brought over. He wouldn't admit it, but he knew young Tabitha was right.

"Now, don't move, Mr. Shadow," she said as she laid out all of her tools.

"Move? Where the heck am I going to move?"

With care, Tabitha grabbed her tools. She gently moved his legs into a more stable position.

"Ouch!" Mr. Shadow wailed. "I thought you were going to slow down!"

"Sorry! Sorry! I just want to do this quickly," Tabitha said. "Just sit still, and it'll all be over soon."

Mr. Shadow grumbled something unrecognizable and folded his front paws. He stuck a piece of bark in his mouth and bit into it to keep himself from screaming.

Tabitha had no prior nursing experience, and it showed. Still, she worked as carefully as she could, placing the two twigs along the backside of Mr. Shadow's hind legs. She then wrapped the legs and the twigs in the newspaper and tied it all together with the shoelaces, only hurting Mr. Shadow twice. Her patient would still be unable to walk, but now his legs would heal properly. She looked proudly at her accomplishment and boasted,

Chapter Twelve

"There, all finished, Mr. Shadow. Now remember," she warned, waving her paw sternly. "Don't try to get up. We'll move you and help you when necessary. In the meantime, just lay here and get some rest." She looked down at him mournfully. "Oh, Mr. Shadow, I wish there was more I could do for you."

"You've done a good job, Nurse Tabitha," Mr. Shadow said kindly. "Now check on the others. I'll be all right for a few minutes."

"Okay. I won't be gone too long," she mumbled. He heard her footsteps vibrating beneath him as she walked away.

Twitch had already shown everyone some high cliffs, scary trees, and a web of deadly spiders by the time Tabitha caught up with them. She met them near a large window at the back of the visitor's building. Inside, there was a gift shop. Statue tee-shirts, statue hats, statue dolls, and suckers lined the shelves while dozens of little statue replicas sat perched in the window front. Tabitha caught her reflection in the glass sitting beside a painting of the great lady. For a moment it almost looked as though Tabitha herself were in that painting, making her feel as tall as the statue. Calvin kept flinching at the sight of his reflection, believing it was a ghoul staring back at him.

"How's Mr. Shadow?" Romeo asked, plucking out handfuls of grass from the ground. "Can he walk yet?"

Tabitha stepped away from the window and her

Life Two

fantasy answering, "No, he can't. His legs are badly broken."

They all bowed their heads.

"I bandaged them though," Tabitha continued. "It just makes me so worried. How will we go on if he can't move?"

"I don't know," Romeo moaned.

"Where should we put him?" Fluffy asked. "I mean, we can't just leave him there in the mud."

"Good point," Tabitha agreed. "I hadn't thought of that."

"We should move him to a dry spot," Romeo suggested.

"But I don't see any," Tabitha said. She looked around at the endless patches of mud.

Twitch held down his left paw hard with his right paw to keep it from twitching. "There's some dry ground near the statue," he suggested. "We could drag him there."

"Drag him? No way!" Tabitha cried with real tears. "That would hurt him far too much."

"How else can we get him there?" Romeo asked.

"I have a big piece of cardboard that I like to lay on sometimes when the ground is too wet," Twitch said. "I could bring it here, and we could put him on it, then slide him over to a better place, sort of like pulling a sled. What do you think?"

"Sounds great!" Tabitha chimed excitedly. The

Life Two

others agreed. Even Calvin.

"Come on, I'll show you the spot I'm thinking of," Twitch said, subtly leaning against his quivering paw.

Everyone followed Twitch. Calvin dragged sluggishly a few feet behind, kicking every rock that crossed his path. He was full of bad attitude and showing his true colors.

Twitch first took them down a long, dirt walkway. It led to the edge of the island and served as a prime photo spot for eager tourists. They stayed there for a moment, taking in the breathtaking sight of the jagged rock wall, and allowed the wind to crash against their faces. Aside from Twitch, none of the Sticks had ever seen water larger than a puddle, let alone an entire ocean. They sat on the pebbles and gravel-covered ground, soaking in the fresh sea air. They wondered, if under more favorable circumstances, whether island life could be great. Was it like the west, a paradise most Sticks dreamed of? Perhaps they would never know. As they sat daydreaming, they thought some more about their families and friends and prayed for the Factory, thinking all the time of the great Bubastis and hoping he was somewhere watching over them.

Fluffy took in a deep breath and beamed, "We should move the Factory here! Whadaya think?"

"No way!" Calvin cried. "Too much water."

"Imagine," Romeo added, "no Alleys."

"Would be nice," Tabitha sighed.

167

Chapter Twelve

"But no Dennis either," Romeo said sadly.

"Why are you guys here in the first place?" Twitch asked. "Are you escaping city life? Looking for a new beginning? In some kind of trouble?"

Tabitha explained their entire situation. She told Twitch about Fidel and the Factory and Twinkle Toes and the note. Twitch hadn't seen Twinkle or Fidel, for that matter, but he did hear a lady screaming from the top of the statue. Perhaps she saw the Alley that placed the note.

"Hey, I'm hungry," Calvin whined, breaking the mood. "That soggy popcorn I found didn't quite do the trick." He gave Twitch a nasty glare.

"Calvin!" Tabitha roared getting in his face. "We have to find a place for Mr. Shadow first! Did you forget about him already?" She squinted her eyes and put one paw to her hip. "You know, if it weren't for you, he probably wouldn't have broken his legs in the first place!"

"Me? Me?" Calvin roared. "What did I do?"

"You know very well you--."

"Stop! Stop it right now!" Twitch yelled, getting between them. "If it's anyone's fault, it's mine. Now, what's done is done. Let's find him a place, then we'll find something for everyone to eat."

Twitch turned and faced Calvin trying to smooth things over. "Why don't we catch some fish? I bet you like fish, don't you Calvin?"

"Fish? *Of course*, I like fish. I'm a cat! Not shark

though. There aren't any hungry sharks...are there?"

"Not that I know of," Twitch said. "Now, it's all settled. We'll help Mr. Shadow, and then I'll get my fishing equipment."

"Wait a minute. You know how to fish?" Fluffy asked, drooling to the ground.

"Yep. It's amazing what you can learn when you're alone."

Mr. Shadow was safely moved on the cardboard sled to the front entrance of the visitor's building without causing him too much discomfort. It was a dry area of concrete covered by a thick awning and far more comfortable than the muddy ground.

"I'll be back in five. Lay back and relax," Twitch said on his way to get his fishing poles. He hobbled off on his can opener leg, disappearing behind the building. The others waited in silence and allowed their stomachs to do the talking. Romeo's growled the loudest.

After ten hungry minutes, Twitch returned with two long, thin branches. Each was curved and had a small plastic bag tied at one end.

"What are those for?" Romeo asked.

"These are my fishing poles," Twitch said proudly. "Here, let me show you how to use them." Twitch explained that the bag on the branch served as a net to catch the small fish that swam near the edge of the island. When he spotted one, he would dunk the bag into the water and scoop it up. The water drained

Chapter Twelve

out of little holes in the bottom of the bag and voila, dinner! "It's not gourmet trout, but these little guys taste just fine. Besides, anything's better than what I got fed at the lab. Two big pills and some dirty water." He picked up the second pole and handed it to Calvin, who had a look of doubt on his face. "Personally, I only catch the dead ones," Twitch added. "I don't like to kill anything, not even fish."

Everyone looked at him funny, like he was from another planet.

"I've seen too many nasty things at the lab, so much pain," Twitch explained. "But, don't mind me. You go right ahead and find yourselves some live ones. Here, Calvin, why don't you give it a try?"

"No thanks, I guess I'm not that hungry after all," Calvin said.

"But I thought you were starving," Tabitha asked. "What's up?"

"I'm going back to Mr. Shadow," he whined. "I'll see you guys later. Have fun at your little fishing party."

Calvin stormed off in a grisly mood. Nobody understood what provoked him this time. "I think he's losing it," Tabitha suggested, watching him walk away through the thick grass. "We're *all* scared. We *all* want to go home. I just wish he knew that. He can be such an ego maniac."

After several clumsy attempts and one accidental plunge in the water, Romeo, Fluffy, Tabitha, and Twitch caught seven tiny orange fish, one for every cat on the island, and one to spare. The seventh one nearly got away. It jumped out of the bag and flew toward the water. Romeo grabbed its slimy body just in time, accidentally squashing it in his paw. Fish guts oozed all over his fur.

"Let's eat one now," Fluffy slurped. "We have an extra one! Calvin and Mr. Shadow will never know!"

Together the cats shared the mini-meal and rubbed their tummies like never before. Twitch put the rest of the fish in an old plastic bag and led everyone back to Mr. Shadow. Calvin was there along with his hot temper.

"My goodness!" Mr. Shadow said with delight. "Who caught all those yummy looking fish?"

"We all did," Romeo said with a half smile and a fish-scented burp.

After the meal, evening had finally come, and the sky turned black. Over the harbor and toward the tall buildings the night sky glowed above its sleepy city. Looming over the island, the great statue stood alone and tall, kissing the stars good night.

Mr. Shadow tried to get some sleep and recommended the others do the same. "Tomorrow's going to be a busy day," he said with a yawn. "If no boats come, we must figure a sure-fire way to get ourselves off of this blasted island."

"But Mr. Shadow," Calvin whimpered, "what if we don't? What if we're stuck here forever, with

Chapter Twelve

nothing but tiny goldfish and that *thing*?" He pointed to Twitch.

"Nonsense," Mr. Shadow scolded. "Stop talking like that, Calvin, and find a place to sleep. I'll see you in the morning."

As the night grew older, strange species of bugs and ugly spiders crept out for their night crawl. Not juicy, meaty spiders, the kind hungry cats look for, but enormous, hairy beasts with fangs and eight strong legs that could wrap around a cat's neck if provoked.

As the cats slept, the insects zigzagged between their ears and around their toes, crunching down for a late night snack. Twitch left the others for his secluded abode and would return at sunrise. Romeo and Fluffy had never slept away from home before. The reality of their situation hit hard that night, along with their desperate feelings of loneliness.

Late into the night, Tabitha woke to find Calvin gone. She searched with her sleepy eyes but was unable to find him, fearing perhaps his anxiety had gotten the best of him. Restless, she got up and decided to hunt for him as the others slept under a cloud of mosquitoes. Along the way, Tabitha escaped the clutches of two prickly spiders as something caught her eye near the water. It was Calvin sitting alone, the crisp wind racing through his fur. Slowly and carefully, Tabitha approached him, startling him as she stepped on a few rocks.

He turned quickly. "Oh, it's you," Calvin

Life Two

muttered, returning his eyes to the blank sea. He dropped his shoulders low.

"Calvin, what's wrong?" Tabitha asked. "Talk to me. You've been out of control all day, and it's starting to scare me."

Calvin looked at the ground and began to fiddle with a pebble. "Nothing. Nothing's wrong."

"It's Twitch, isn't it?" Tabitha guessed. "I know he's odd, *very* odd, but he's harmless. He just wants some friends. Besides, he's going to help us, that's what Mr. Shadow says."

"No, it's not that. It's not that at all." He kicked the rock into the water. "I told you, it's nothing."

"Is it that audition?"

Calvin shook his head and began to cry like a baby right there on the rocks.

"Oh Calvin, you'll see, starting tomorrow Mr. Shadow will figure a way to get us out of here. And who knows, maybe a ferry will come, or maybe Waffles and Vittles will come back. Now, don't you think you ought to get some sleep?"

Calvin struggled to clear his throat and finally asked, "Tabitha?"

"Yes?"

"What do you think happened to Twinkle Toes? I mean, if he's not here, where is he? Where could he be?"

Tabitha sighed and stared at the stars. She realized she hadn't thought of Twinkle Toes for many

173

Chapter Twelve

hours. "I wish I knew, Calvin. But don't worry, we'll find him as soon as we get home." She looked back at him and said, "You know, I've never seen this side of you. I didn't even know you cared about Toes that much."

"Yeah, well," Calvin said, "just don't tell the others."

The two Sticks laughed for a moment realizing what good friends they were after all. She knew Calvin would always be difficult to be around, that was just his nature. But Tabitha also knew deep down there lived a sensitive, caring cat. She would never forget their moments together by the sea.

That night as Tabitha lay on the cold concrete she wondered if all she told Calvin was really true. Would they really find a way back home? She finally shut her eyes, convincing herself of it. It had to be true. It simply had to.

Chapter Thirteen

Back in the deep, dark depths of the city near 57th and 6th, Fidel twiddled his tags. Beside him were Bait and Jailbird, the new guy. Jailbird was asleep from too much nip. He had passed out right on Fidel's floor. Bait stared at him nervously.

"What are we gonna do, boss?" Bait asked.

"What are you talking about?" Fidel snapped.

"Jailbird? He's been passed out for hours."

Fidel reached behind him and grabbed an old, dried orange peel. He cupped it in his paw and ground it in Jailbird's nose.

"Yuck!" Jailbird shouted, bouncing out of his slumber.

"There!" Fidel said. "That's what we're gonna do."

Jailbird stood up and wobbled around the alley.

Chapter Thirteen

Disoriented, he stumbled and bumped into boxes and garbage cans, knocking one completely on its side. Then, he numbly headed for the street.

"Hey, Bird?" Fidel called. "Just where do you think you're goin'?" Fidel ran a cigarette butt under his nose and smelled its sweet scent. "Come on back here. I've got somethin' for you."

Jailbird gave Fidel a tired look and slowly stepped back into the alley. Bait giggled and laughed in the corner, counting the number of scattered mouse skulls lying around.

"Bait!" Fidel yelled. "Give our new friend some more stuff. He looks like he needs it."

"Whatever you say, boss," Bait shrugged. He knocked one of the skulls out of his way and grabbed a pawful of nip from the ground.

"And none for you!" Fidel warned.

Bait looked back at him. "Awe, come on! Just one little taste?" he begged.

"No!" Fidel roared.

"Pleeease?" Bait tried again, showing off all his gray teeth.

"No!" Fidel howled, slamming his paw to the wall. "Now get on with it!"

"All right, all right," Bait conceded. He took the nip over to Jailbird who swayed left to right, bobbing his head and closing his eyes. "Open wide, JB," Bait said, shoving some nip in Jailbird's mouth. "Just what ya need to perk up."

Life Two

Chapter Thirteen

Jailbird's face scrunched from the potent smell of the catnip. The wadful on his tongue was quickly dissolved into his throat. He slapped it around inside his mouth, making gagging and coughing noises.

"Good boy, Jailbird," Fidel said with a grin. "Eat up! It's good for you. Trust me."

Bits of nip stuck to Bait's paw. He casually brought them to his face when Fidel wasn't looking. Feeling victorious, he slowly stuck out his tongue and began to lick the intoxicating herb.

"What did I tell you?" Fidel screamed, wrapping his paw tightly around Bait's neck, turning his lips marble blue. Bait's tongue jutted out of his mouth like a spear. Fidel scraped the green off with a jagged piece of wood and threw Bait to the ground. "That'll teach you to disobey me! Stay off that stuff!"

Bait coughed and wailed on his belly. Little nicks from the wood dotted his tongue, and the tiny specs of nip blew away like dust.

Fidel watched, rubbing his paws together as the effects of the nip swirled through Jailbird's blood. His weary and frazzled face quickly lit up like a circus. His legs straightened with a burst of energy, and his eyes shot wide open. A smile bigger than a car slapped across his face, and he started laughing maniacally.

"Now, that's more like it, Jailbird," Fidel snickered. "Let's go find us something to eat."

"Hee-hee-hee," Jailbird cackled, his body shaking with a rattling energy. "Food!" he gleamed.

Life Two

Bait still lay on the ground examining his tongue and rubbing his neck. Fidel grabbed the fur patch atop his head and yelled, "Come on, Bait! We're going!" He ripped him from the ground and tossed him forward. Bait landed on all fours, nearly slipping on a banana peel. Fidel spit and led them out of the alley.

Out on the street Fidel walked like a king. He held his head high and squinted his eyes. Behind him scurried Bait and Jailbird. Bait lackadaisically walked in Fidel's wake, bumping into mailboxes and newspaper stands, his tongue hanging low. Jailbird pranced with a jitter, giggling at everything he saw. He was completely wasted.

"What's all that racket back there?" Fidel thundered. Bait and Jailbird shrugged their shoulders. "Keep it quiet! I won't have you two acting like idiots around me."

Fidel continued his strut through the city. As he marched down the sidewalk, squirrels and other common street animals dashed out of his way or hid under boxes and crates. They shook nervously when he sauntered by, then slyly peeked out to watch 'his majesty' walk on. Because of his latest conquest over the sticks, the Alleys bowed to him as he passed their corners and hideouts. Oozes of respect and amazement exuded from the males, while the females swooned breathlessly, their little hearts a flutter. Fidel was a killer in more ways than one.

A few minutes into their walk, Bait noticed

Chapter Thirteen

a small family of mice scurrying ahead. He showed Fidel immediately.

"Good work, Bait. Let's get 'em!"

In two seconds the cats charged after the mice. Mom, dad, and three little juniors raced down the sidewalk, panting their tails off. They sped down 57th, passed 58th and 59th, all the way to City Park. Avoiding the open space of the park, the mice quickly darted down an alley. They ran in circles finding not so much as a crack in a wall. All the pipes were rusted shut, and hiding in the garbage cans would only prolong the inevitable. Fidel, Bait, and the disoriented Jailbird had them cornered. Fidel stood framed in the entrance, billows of smoke hovering around his body like demons. He huffed and hissed as the mice frantically continued their hopeless search. It seemed the rodents were doomed. They stood still.

Slowly, the three cats crept deeper and deeper toward their prey, walking together as a brick wall. The little mice before them tippy-toed backwards, eye-to-eye with their killers. Their little white ears shivered and shook, as their bodies crouched lower and lower to the ground. Fidel stopped walking and raised his paw with a devilish sneer. This was it, and the mice knew it. They shut their eyes tightly and gulped hard. Fidel had them right where he wanted them.

Suddenly, Bait lunged forward with a roar and leapt for the mice family. This startled them so much that they flung back into the air and frantically scurried

Life Two

around completely out of control. Fidel hissed, keeping his hot, angry eyes on Bait. Without a blink, Fidel sunk his paw into a mouse's tail as it tried to scamper around. The mouse clawed and clawed at the ground but got nowhere.

"Help!" he squealed from under Fidel's paw. "Help!"

Another mouse saw what had happened and immediately ran to his aid, but it was too late. Fidel had him dangling right in front of his gruesome face. The tiny mouse hung from his tail, twisting and squirming. He covered his little black eyes with his paws and wailed. The other mice watched in agony as the one slowly disappeared into Fidel's mouth. He could see the small lump of his body slide down his throat and out of sight.

"Nooo!" he screamed, pounding the ground. But he wouldn't have much time to wallow. Bait instantly scooped him up and stuffed him into his drooling mouth, crunching his little bones with his sharp teeth. Fidel looked behind him and saw two more mouse tails dangling from Jailbird's lips. Jailbird grinned and sucked them in like strands of spaghetti.

Then it was over. A tasty meal, a loud burp, and everyone was happy, but not for long. "Blast!" Fidel yelled throwing down his paw. One mouse had gotten away. "Let's get out of here," Fidel growled. "I need a drink."

The three cats slithered away and headed for

Chapter Thirteen

Smelly's. The dark alley sat still and silent once again. Then a tiny mouse cry could be heard. Near the back of the alley under an old sneaker hid little Frank. He clutched onto the shoelaces that surrounded him and wept into the sweaty sole. He was lost forever and had no idea where to go. His whole family had just been eaten by a bunch of cats, and he saw the whole thing.

Chapter Fourteen

The next morning a hazy sun wrapped itself in a robe of dark clouds and gently tapped Romeo awake with a single drop of rain. Romeo opened his sleepy eyes to find himself still on the island. It wasn't all a dream. Home remained a lifetime away. He groggily stretched out his hind legs and yawned wide enough to hold the entire statue. Scratching a row of bug bites planted on his back, he glared off into space. In the near distance he could see Mr. Shadow still asleep at the building entrance, with Tabitha and Fluffy nearby. Calvin was nowhere to be seen. Romeo figured he'd better take a look around before anyone else woke up.

Romeo explored the outside of the building, stomping through dead leaves and twisted weeds. His insides ached at the sight of the endless sea. In his jaws he carried a twig to drag through the dirt. He stumbled

Chapter Fourteen

to the edge of the island and took a long look at the city near the horizon. It looked peaceful and quiet and almost pretty. If only he could always see the city as he did that day. His eyes drifted up to the statue. He looked at her with a wink.

Romeo quickly found himself deeper into the island, far away from his friends. The further he got, the creepier the plants and the eerier the sounds. He cautiously slowed his pace. In the sky he saw two angry birds fighting frantically over a lizard. They squawked and squeaked and tore the reptile to bits. Romeo licked his lips in hunger.

As he wandered on, Romeo stayed in view of the water. He knew he could follow the shore back to the others. He found a patch of huge, rugged rocks. They were all different sizes and shapes. Some sparkled like a new ring, some were a myriad of colors and textures. One even looked like a hippo. The rocks rested in the muddy sand as the water crashed against their sharp edges. Romeo ran excitedly toward them like he had just found a hidden playground. With all his might he leapt up to the top of the highest rock and danced in the murky sun. For the first time since their arrival, he found something to enjoy.

Romeo hopped from rock to rock, climbing up the sides like he was a chameleon. Then, something caught his eye. It was a shark, a freshly dead shark. It lay there bobbing in the water between two boulders. A small puddle of red liquid floated nearby. Its two

Life Two

deep, black eyes bugged from their sockets. Tiny sea creatures circled the carcass, nibbling on the decaying flesh. Romeo clung onto the slippery rock and peered over its side for a closer look. The shark was ten cats long with monstrously sharp teeth and gray, leathery skin. It had obviously been attacked by something, perhaps a boat propeller. A huge, bloody gash ripped across its stomach showing off the ocean king's squishy insides.

Romeo stepped off the rock to get a closer look, but he slipped. His body flung into the cold water right in front of the shark's ghostly face. Romeo screamed and wailed and tread water with all his might. The motion of the current pushed his little body right into the shark's mouth, sharp teeth all around him. It smelled something awful inside the big fish. Romeo panicked. He flailed out of control, splashing bloody water all around him as his body was sucked deeper and deeper into the shark's open, dead mouth. He quickly grabbed a large, cracked tooth, saving himself from being completely drawn in. From where he hung, he could barely see the outside world. As Romeo held onto that tooth it started to crumble in his paw. He hurriedly pulled with all his might and heaved himself up to another tooth, ripping the first one from its gums. He grabbed that one and another and slowly walked himself through the mouth back into the water. Romeo brushed some shark guts off and managed to hoist himself onto the rocks. Once safe, he lay there like a

Chapter Fourteen

beached whale, completely in shock over his creepy mishap.

Suddenly, Romeo heard a noise and turned to face the bushes. His tail bloomed as he crouched low. Was it Twitch? Was it something else? Something scary? The shark's angry ghost?

"Calvin!" Romeo yelled, relieved as he spotted Calvin's familiar yellow and orange tail swaying at the bottom of a shrub. "What are you doing in there?" But Calvin didn't answer.

"Calvin, I know it's you! Now, come out. What are you doing here?" Romeo asked again, this time poking his nose into the brush.

Unnoticed, Calvin slipped out the other end and snuck up behind Romeo. "Boo!" he yelled, pulling Romeo's tail.

Romeo let out a tremendous scream. "Calvin!" he roared. "What do you think you're doing?"

"Awe, come on, Romeo," he teased. "Admit it. It was funny." Calvin's nose caught a whiff of Romeo's stinky fur. "Jeez, you sure smell funky. What have you been into?"

Romeo plucked a chunk of shark vein off his shoulder. "Whatever, Calvin," he muttered. "So, tell me, Mr. Scaredy cat, why are you out and about by yourself?"

Calvin lay on his back and playfully rolled in the dirt. "Well, I was hungry so I thought I'd look for some food."

Life Two

"I found a dead shark!" Romeo exclaimed. "You could eat that!"

"Yeah, right," Calvin chuckled. "You just happened to find a dead shark. Quit pulling my leg." Calvin held out his paw and showed Romeo several ruby red berries he found hidden in the bush. "I found these!"

Romeo squinted. "I don't know, Calvin. You should ask Mr. Shadow before you eat those. I remember Mrs. Crumb telling Dennis not to eat any mysterious berries when he went on his camping trip. If you ask me, those berries look mysterious. Besides, shark meat is..."

"Quit it, already. I don't believe you," Calvin said with an air of doubt. "But, if it'll make you happy, I'll go ask Mr. Shadow about the berries. Then you can show me your little shark."

Romeo and Calvin ventured back to Mr. Shadow and the others. Everyone was awake and covered in plenty of itchy bug bites. Soon Twitch had returned as well. He sat beside Mr. Shadow, his injured legs looking no better.

"Oh, *he's* here. I wish he'd leave us alone," Calvin whined, spotting Twitch a few feet away.

Tabitha shot him a nasty look.

"Calvin," Romeo snapped. "I don't understand you sometimes. Twitch has been helping us ever since we got to this lousy place and all you've done is complain about him. I just don't get it."

Chapter Fourteen

"Yeah, well," Calvin whispered. "There's something I don't trust about that guy. He's up to something, I know it. He's anti-actor. That must be it."

"Calvin, you're impossible. He's *not* going to eat us, and he's *not* going to kill us, and he certainly doesn't have it in for actors!" Romeo thundered, running toward the others.

Up ahead, Tabitha warned Mr. Shadow of a grisly situation.

"Look out, Mr. Shadow!" she screamed. "It's one of those creepy spiders again. It's crawling your way!"

Mr. Shadow turned and sure enough, inching up a twig was a huge, hairy arachnid, its body practically as big as Romeo's head.

"Hurry!" Get it away from me!" Mr. Shadow squirmed. "Kill it! Somebody kill it!"

He wiggled around and tried to shoo the bug away with one of his broken legs. "Ouch!" he wailed. "Help!"

"I'm not going to kill it," Twitch announced as the spider's segmented legs moved higher up Mr. Shadow's body.

"Do something somebody!" Tabitha yelled.

As soon as the spider reached Mr. Shadow's yellow knit sweater, Mr. Shadow's eyes rolled back into his head and he passed out.

Romeo grabbed a thick branch and swung

as hard as he could. The hungry spider sailed like a baseball over a wall of trees. Romeo gleamed boastfully. "Got him."

"We better be careful, though," Twitch warned. "He'll be back, and with his friends, too. They always seem to return with a friend."

Tabitha shrugged her shoulders and began to fan Mr. Shadow awake.

Calvin jumped in with the berries clutched tightly in his paw. "Look what I found!" he shouted, waving the berries in everyone's face. "There's a whole bush of them right over there." He pointed at the shrubs.

Mr. Shadow grunted and attempted to sit up. "Ouch!" When certain the giant spider was gone, he said, "Calvin, bring those over here. I want to take a good look."

Calvin walked up to Mr. Shadow and handed him a berry. "Don't they look yummy?" he said with delight.

Mr. Shadow inspected the berry very carefully. He cracked it open and smelled its fruitful juice. "Yes," he finally said. "It does look and smell delicious but--."

Just then, Twitch overheard what was going on. "Oh no! Don't eat *those*!" he warned. "Those are poisonous berries!"

"He may be right, Calvin," Mr. Shadow agreed. "They could be poison, *poison*!"

Chapter Fourteen

"Come on, Calvin," Fluffy motioned. "Throw those away. Let's catch some more fish."

"And shark! I found a dead shark!" Romeo bragged.

Calvin eyed everyone skeptically. "Hey guys, you're not going to believe Twitch, are you? A cat we just met? Did you ever think that maybe he just wants all the berries for himself? Maybe he's going to stuff them into our dead bodies and make cat pie! Did you ever think of that?"

"That's ridiculous, Calvin," Tabitha said. "Put the berries down!"

"No!" he roared, lifting the pawful high above his head. With a grin, he slowly lowered them to his mouth teasingly, when Twitch jumped up and knocked them out of his clutches.

"I said don't eat them!" Twitch insisted.

"Just watch me!" Calvin yelled defiantly. "You're not my boss!" He picked up the fallen berries from the ground and quickly stuffed them in his mouth, chewing fast. He gobbled them to bits with a snide little grin, savoring each tasty morsel.

Everyone stood back and waited for something terrible to happen.

"See?" Calvin said proudly. "Poisonous berries. Nothing to worry about." As he spoke he rapidly grew greener and greener. His whiskers curled up, and his nose flared. Calvin grabbed his throat with his two front paws as his eyes bulged. His cheeks puffed way

Life Two

out, and his ears folded in half. Suddenly, he fell to the ground, writhing and convulsing. Then, his mouth sprung open and a single berry pit shot out like a cannon. Calvin started to breath heavily and squirmed deep into the dirt. He clutched his stomach and bit his tail hard. For a brief agonizing moment he looked up, then collapsed like a dead bear.

Tabitha rushed to his side. "Calvin! Is he dead?" she cried. "Oh no, tell me he's not dead! He can't be! He just can't!"

Fluffy followed behind her and quickly put his ear to Calvin's chest. "He's not dead. He's still breathing."

Tabitha sighed with relief.

Unconscious, Calvin lay pathetically drooling and snoring in the mud.

"Actually," Twitch started to speak, but Mr. Shadow cut him off.

"How dare he not listen to me!" Mr. Shadow screamed. "I told him not to eat those blasted berries! Now look at him. Between him and me and our eight-legged friend, we'll never get out of here! *Never!*"

"Sure we will, Mr. Shadow," Fluffy encouraged. "Waffles and Vittles will come back for us, I know it!"

"But what if they don't?" Romeo asked nervously. "We can't rely on that. Come on. Didn't we learn about survival in combat class? If we put our heads together, we can find another way off this island. It could be weeks before Waffles and Vittles return.

Chapter Fourteen

What will happen to Twinkle Toes by then?"

Fluffy paced and ranted. "We can't think about all that now. Just look at the city, Romeo! It's too far away for us to swim, and there's just no other way out! We have no choice but to wait for them!"

"No!" Romeo cried. "I'm not going to wait! I have to get back to Dennis and Twinkle Toes and the Factory! If you want to wait, wait without me!"

"Fine!" Fluffy barked.

The two Sticks stood back-to-back, paws folded, huffing. Mr. Shadow finally intervened. "Look males, fighting among ourselves is going to get us nowhere. Everyone's cranky, and we all need to settle down. Now, if there is another way out of here, we need to find it. I think you should all walk around together and try to find something, anything, that could help us get home." All of a sudden, a gust of wind crashed through the area and dumped massive amounts of soggy leaves onto Mr. Shadow.

"I'm not going anywhere with *him*!" Fluffy said in Romeo's direction.

"That's fine with me!" Romeo scowled back.

"You know, Romeo," Fluffy glared, "this is all your fault! We wouldn't be in this mess if it wasn't for you and your stupid family problems! It's you who Fidel really wants!"

"Well, I...I- " Romeo sucked in his bottom lip and charged off.

Tabitha watched in horror. "Now, look what

Life Two

you've done!" she barked. "That was down right cruel!"

Fluffy kicked a rock and dropped his head low. It was obvious the tensions of the situation were testing some old friendships.

"Now what are we supposed to do?" Tabitha asked angrily.

Mr. Shadow struggled to knock the leaves out of his way and out of his mouth. "All right," he mumbled, spitting out a twig. "Just explore by yourselves! We'll deal with this matter later. And don't come back until you've found something. You hear me? Until you've *found something*!"

Fluffy watched Tabitha race off to join Romeo. "Fine! Go with *him*!" he yelped, darting off in the other direction.

"You shouldn't go that way, Fluffy!" Twitch warned. "It's dangerous down there!"

"Leave me alone!" Fluffy shouted back.

Twitch shook his pink and green head and walked away. During all the arguing, he had forgotten to tell the others to look for a special flower he had heard about that would cure Calvin of the berries. Without it, he'd only grow sicker and sicker until his toes shrunk and his lungs exploded. He quite possibly could even lose a life. Twitch would spend the morning searching for just that flower knowing it was hidden in some secret, dangerous location.

After about an hour, everyone returned tired

Chapter Fourteen

and worn out. Fluffy and Romeo still refused to even look at each other. It drove Mr. Shadow nuts.

With his vast island knowledge and skill, Twitch hadn't found the healing plant for Calvin, who was looking mighty peaked. Tabitha did find a scrap of paper and an old soda bottle. With a piece of bark, she wrote an S.O.S. message on the paper, stuffed it in the bottle and sent it sailing on its way. It was a long shot at best. Mr. Shadow fell asleep covered in bird droppings. Calvin was still out cold.

"He's burning up," cried Tabitha, feeling Calvin's forehead. "He's getting worse, and his toes are shaking."

"I've heard there's a special flower with petals that have medicinal healing powers," Twitch announced. "It's the only way to make Calvin better."

"Why didn't you tell us that before we went searching around the island?" Fluffy snapped.

"Because," Twitch said, "you and Romeo were acting like idiots, and I couldn't get a word in! Maybe if we all cooperate, we--."

"All right! All right!" Romeo butted in and stepping forward. "Look, considering our predicament, I am officially taking over. It's obvious we are getting nowhere fast. Clearly, Mr. Shadow isn't able to lead us right now, I mean, just look at him. He's pathetic!"

Mr. Shadow's nose was covered in bird doo, and it was even starting to slide toward his mouth. Romeo flicked a steaming heap of it away and continued.

Life Two

"Until he's better, what I say goes." He finished his sentence proudly with his snout to the air.

"What?" Fluffy growled. "Are you kidding? Who made you king?" He looked at Tabitha. "Come on, Tab, you're not in favor of this, are you?"

She turned her head away.

"So?" Romeo asked. "What's it gonna be?" He stood on top of Mr. Shadow's belly and tapped his paw waiting for an answer.

"I'm outta here!" Fluffy hollered. "I'll find that flower, and then we'll see who's boss!"

"Don't go that way!" Twitch called. "Remember, it's dangerous!" He scratched his two tails and watched Fluffy storm off. "You don't even know what the flower looks like!"

"Just leave him be," Romeo said. "There's no talking to him now. I say we look around for that plant ourselves."

Tabitha agreed with her new island leader. Twitch described in detail what to look for. "It's a blue flower with green dots on the tips of the pedals. Its about the size of a daisy and grows under the elephant trees."

"Elephant trees?" Romeo asked. "What are those?"

"Elephant trees are a group of trees that together look like a giant elephant. There aren't many around here. They were cut down because...because..."

"Because what?" Tabitha asked nervously.

195

Chapter Fourteen

"Because," Twitch began, "supposedly they are alive!"

Romeo rolled his eyes. "So!" he laughed. "All plants are alive. Mr. Sox taught me that."

"They're not alive the way other plants are," Twitch explained. "It's like they've got minds of their own. Like you."

"No way!" Romeo snapped. "That's crazy! That's the most ridiculous thing I've ever heard. Whoever told you that was pulling your leg."

"Hey, that's just what I've heard. I can't say if it's really true, but I can't say if it isn't. I will say, I've often heard strange noises at night."

"All right, all right," Romeo snapped annoyed. "Let's just get going already. Calvin is looking worse by the second."

Twitch hobbled off in one direction and Romeo in another.

"Romeo," Tabitha called, running up behind him. "Can I go with you? I don't want to walk alone."

"Sure," Romeo mumbled. "As long as you're not afraid of the *elephant trees*!" He screeched in a spooky voice, standing on his hind legs and waving his paws in the air like a demon. "Booo!"

Together they giggled and teased for the first time all day and journeyed off in search of a rare plant and a miracle. After an hour, they hadn't found either.

About fifteen minutes into his search, Fluffy realized he didn't know what he was looking for. He knew nothing of the elephant tree tale, or the flower for that matter, and felt absolutely sick at the thought of Romeo being in charge. *The nerve*, he said to himself. *I should be the leader. I'll show them who the real hero is.* He took all that anxious energy and picked up every flower and weed he could find and stuffed them under his collar. Surely one of them would be the right one. That would show everyone.

Fluffy soon reached the far edge of the island, the farthest point from where he began and the supposedly dangerous spot Twitch had warned of, though Fluffy didn't see why. It looked the same as any other place, same bushes, same mud, same discarded candy wrappers and gunk.

"That Twitch is crazy," Fluffy thought. "Anyone who's been through as many lab experiments as him has got to be crazy."

After another few minutes of wandering around in the pattering drizzle, Fluffy stumbled onto something quite unusual. Behind a cracked, concrete bench was what seemed to be a large hole about four cats wide. Its rough rim was speckled with rocks and dirt and an odd, unrecognizable smell came from inside. Fluffy stood at the edge and peered down, fearing some large sea creature might rise up and attack him. He hesitantly stuck his nose inside and sniffed, wind whipping through him like a ghost. Eerie swooshing noises echoed in and out of the hole as a tornado of dirt and dust began to swarm around him. Fluffy lost

Chapter Fourteen

his balance and slipped, knocking his butt and supply of flowers to the ground. His back paws slid into the earth as his front paws clung tightly to a weed jetting out from the mud. He prayed with all his might to Bubastis that the weed would magically sprout up to the sky and lift him to safety. He wiggled his back legs and struggled and shook, but gravity pulled his body down the hole. His front paws frantically grabbed at the dirt as they slipped out of sight.

Across the island, Romeo and Tabitha were kicking rocks to each other.

"Ouch!" Tabitha cried. "That hurt!" She grabbed a rock and aimed for Romeo's front paw. Whack! She snapped her tail to the rock sending it careening in Romeo's direction.

"Hey! Quit it!" Romeo whined. The ammo hit his leg knocking him to the ground with a thud. His leg pounded something awful.

"Sorry," Tabitha said with a giggle.

Romeo clutched his throbbing leg and moaned like a real drama queen. He continued his whine-fest long after the pain stopped, trying to plague Tabitha with heavy doses of guilt.

"It's not working," she teased. "I know you're fine."

Romeo smirked.

"Come on, we've got to find the hippo trees," she reminded him.

Life Two

"Elephant trees!" Romeo said with a punch in his voice.

Tabitha rolled her girly eyes. "Oh, whatever. You know what I mean."

Together Romeo and Tabitha scoured the west side of the island. It was completely empty except for two crumbling stone benches and used tubes of film buried in the mud. The statue's chiseled nose and chin provided a cool blanket of shade to the day's painfully humid temperatures and intermittent drizzle.

Romeo had about given up when he heard Tabitha yell, "Hey, Romeo! Come look at this!"

He followed her voice to a patch of old, but ordinary trees, about ten or so. They were round and tall and covered with leaves. Romeo walked in circles around the mini-forest calling, "Tabitha? Where are you?"

Just then, Tabitha's paw jutted out between two of the trees and yanked Romeo inside a private forest.

Romeo pushed her off. "Where are we?"

"I don't know, Romeo, but look." She pointed to a series of tall trees that together oddly formed what looked like an elephant. The bark on the trees was covered by an oozing, gray sap. It was dotted with dead birds and rodents who chose the wrong trees to call home. Romeo's heart stopped.

"Is that? Is that?" he asked nervously.

Tabitha nodded her head.

"Maybe we should get Twitch," Romeo

Chapter Fourteen

Life Two

suggested. "After all, he knows more about these trees than anyone."

"No way," Tabitha said with a grin. "He couldn't even find them in all the time he's been on this island. Let's check it out for ourselves. Besides, we don't have much time to waste." She followed a lone eyeball as it slid down the slime. It nearly gagged her. "I'm a little scared, but Calvin needs that flower."

"But they're...alive," Romeo remarked.

"Don't be ridiculous!" Tabitha teased. "Trees don't have minds of their own. Cats do. Besides, those trees look more dead than a patch of weeds. Come on! Follow me!"

She pulled Romeo's tail and brought him closer to the mysterious trees. Romeo could feel hundreds of goose bumps waking up under his fur. He gulped as his friend darted to the base of a big, scary trunk. It grew from the ground as wide as a house.

"Catch me if you can!" Tabitha smirked. She ran around to the back of the tree where she couldn't be seen.

Romeo stood there alone. It suddenly got very dark, almost as if the trees moved closer together. He waited in the mud for Tabitha to come out the other side, and when she didn't, he yelled, "Come on, Tabitha! Stop fooling around! Tabitha? You're gonna get it when we get out of here," he said angrily. He took a deep, slow breath and stepped toward the trees. The sap started to ooze faster and drip heavier onto the dirty ground. The closer he got the more his insides turned.

"Tabitha?" he asked again in a whisper. "Come on, you win." He cautiously looked up at the massive trees looming above him like a monster. "Tabitha, you're really making me mad. Don't you remember what Mr. Shadow taught us? Always stay together."

Just then, Romeo heard a low, breathy moan. "Come to the tree," it said. in the slowest voice possible.

Romeo's fur stood up on end. He crouched to the ground and wanted to cry, but dared not. After all, he was a leader now. "Who...who said that?"

"Come to the tree!" It said again like an old ghost.

"I don't want to!" Romeo flung himself down and hid under his front paws.

"I said, come to the tree or you'll *never* see your pretty friend *ever* again!"

"But...but..."

"*Now!*"

Shaking, Romeo inched his way closer to the talking trees. Twitch was right. They were alive. And they didn't like Romeo.

At the trunk Romeo heard, "Close your eyes!"

Romeo nervously did as he was told and held tightly to his tail. He wondered if he would be torn to bits. Drowned in sap? Gagged with leaves?

"Now, open you eyes slowly," the tree ordered

with a rustle of its leaves.

Romeo did.

"Boo!" Tabitha yelled.

"Ahhh!" Romeo screamed as he flung into the air, then slid back down the tree. "Tabitha?" he yelled in a panic.

"Ah-ha!" Tabitha laughed before him. "Gotcha!"

Romeo's blood boiled out of control. "Why, I oughta kill you!" His chest heaved violently up and down, and his lips pursed together. He had never been so angry with her.

"Oh, get over it, Romeo," Tabitha snickered. "These are just a bunch of big old trees. You should've seen the look on your face when you--"

Suddenly, the large trunk branch swung down like a huge arm and grabbed Tabitha right off the ground. It knotted itself around like a pretzel with Tabitha wrapped in the middle. The branch flung her up and down and side to side to dizzying heights. It swirled her in and out of the canopy of leaves fast and with more loops than the most dangerous roller coaster ride. She was covered in her own barf and sliced by the myriad of twigs.

"Whooo!" she wailed. "Help!"

Romeo watched from the ground in horror as Tabitha whipped through the air like a rag doll. He gnawed at his claws and hid behind a rock. After a moment, a branch from another tree and another and another joined in the game. Pretty soon, all the trees were playing a maniacal game of catch with Tabitha, tossing her from tree to tree. Just then, the main branch did something amazing. It filled itself with air, bent backwards, and shot Tabitha out over the wall of trees. She soared through the air like a shooting star, landing with a crunch. The other trees clapped and gave each other high fives with their branches and returned to their original, unassuming, still positions.

Romeo ran to Tabitha with little hope of finding her alive. What if she were dead? How would he get her out of there? What would he tell the others?

After a moment of searching, he finally found his friend. His worst nightmare was realized. She was dead. Her pretty yellow fur lay against her soft skin in a matted mess. A trail of blood followed the trees all the way to where she landed. Beside her was a small supply of green flowers with blue tips. Romeo stood above her. He gently closed her eyes with his paw and waited, tears streaming down his face.

The creepy patch of trees just stood there, almost looking at him like some eerie painting. Romeo tried not to look, afraid they'd jump out of their roots and kill him too. He hid behind Tabitha's body as close to the ground as he could. The reality that Tabitha had lost a life came to him as he stared off into the stars. They floated above in an ocean of mystery, pale and empty. Romeo blinked and blinked and the stars grew dimmer and dimmer. He thought they looked sad, like

Life Two

he was. He wondered, did stars ever feel lonely way up there? Their hazy glow bounced off Tabitha's shiny collar, and Romeo felt her death. He waited in his anger until she finally awoke.

"What happened?" she said groggily, lifting her sore head. "Romeo? Is that you?"

"Yes," he answered somberly. "I'm here."

Romeo told Tabitha the sad truth about what happened. They talked it over and agreed not to tell anyone just yet. Too much was happening to deal with a death, and such a bizarre one at that. It would only drain everyone's hope, and hope was in short supply already. Still, Tabitha was as sad as sad can be.

Twenty minutes later, she was physically feeling slightly better. She looked at the haunting trees and immediately remembered the flowers and their purpose. "Let's take them to Calvin." She bolted with the stars reflecting in her eyes.

"Yes! Let's!" Romeo agreed.

The two cats took one last look at the trees and dashed away. They were soon back with Mr. Shadow and Calvin. During his nap Mr. Shadow had drooled himself into a puddle and was presently trying to clean off his fur, though he could only turn his head slightly to one side. "Romeo," he called spotting the young male coming his way. "You may have to help me bathe myself later. You don't mind, do you?" he asked with a tongue full of matted fur.

Romeo peered down Shadow's gooey body and

swallowed hard, a big lump in his throat. "Uh, mind?" he said with a gasp. "Well, let's just see how you feel later. Maybe you won't need my help after all."

"Very well," Mr. Shadow replied.

Romeo turned his back to Mr. Shadow and pretended to barf. Twitch chuckled as subtly as he could.

Calvin was still very hot, and the skin beneath his fur was getting damp and sweaty. Clearly, he was worse. Twitch lay beside him and stroked his head.

"Where on earth did you find those flowers?" Twitch asked feeling a rumble come over his body.

Tabitha cocked her head to one side. "We, uh, found them under a bush," she trembled. "Yeah, that's it, under a bush." She glared at Romeo.

"She's right," Romeo said. "We found them under a bush. I guess you were wrong about the elephant trees."

Twitch stared down at Calvin's quivering body. He was all curled up into a ball on a soft bed of leaves. "Well," Twitch sighed, "it's good you found the plant, but...he's been out awfully long. It may be too late to bring him back."

"But, the plant has got to work! It's just got to! I went through hell for these flowers!" Tabitha cried. When she talked her head moved and pinched a nerve. "Ouch!" she screamed.

"What's the matter with you?" Mr. Shadow asked.

Life Two

"Nothing, I...I must have stepped on a rock."

"I thought you just found these under a bush!" Twitch pestered on.

"Yeah, it was just such a prickly bush," Tabitha sighed.

Mr. Shadow sat up from his drool spot. "Anyway, Calvin won't die, will he? I mean, lose a life?"

Twitch nodded his funny head in a way different from his regular bobbing. "Yes, he could lose a life."

"But we have tons of plants!" Tabitha cried again. "Won't that keep him alive?"

"We just have to wait and see," Twitch said. "If he does lose a life, he will keep dying. The flowers can't help him once too much time has passed."

"Well, what are we waiting for?" Romeo growled. "Let's feed him the flower now! Shove it in his ears if you have to!"

Calvin's drugged state found his tongue hanging low outside of his mouth and his eyes shut tight. Twitch nervously dug his leg into the mud. Tabitha handed Romeo several of the potent blue and green petals.

"Stuff two of them into his mouth," Twitch explained.

Romeo nodded. With his paw he carefully placed two of the richer pedals under Calvin's rough tongue as Tabitha held his head. She and Romeo leaned back and waited for a miracle. Calvin just lay

Chapter Fourteen

there drooling.

"What's supposed to happen, Twitch?" Romeo asked. "He's not moving!"

"Hmmm," Twitch said. "You're right. He doesn't seem to be responding." He rubbed his chin with his good paw.

"What do you *mean,* he's not responding?" Mr. Shadow demanded. "Do something else!"

"I'm sorry, but I don't know what I *can* do. He's looped out of his mind."

Tabitha began to cry frantically and ran to Romeo. Romeo tried to remain calm and fight the memories that were brewing in his head. The thought of losing another friend, and so soon, was inconceivable. He wouldn't allow it. Not like this. He quickly took another petal and shoved it into Calvin's mouth, and another, and another. Twitch hadn't even noticed for he was too busy trying to dislodge his leg from the mud.

Then, like bacon on a Sunday morning, something started to sizzle. It was a thick, gooey mess coming from Calvin's mouth soaking his fur in a bubbly ooze. His throat gurgled and burped as though it had a mind of its own. Instantly, Tabitha and Romeo jumped back, their knees rattling. Calvin's body trembled and quivered on the ground scaring a little worm right out of his home. His eyes rolled around in his head, though he still seemed unconscious.

"Calvin!" Romeo yelled. "Can you hear me?"

Life Two

Wake up! Wake up!" But Calvin only saw hallucinatory pictures in his head.

Inside Calvin's head the outside world disappeared, and he began to swirl into a haze of shadows and colors. Bright blobs of blues, yellows, and purples floated around him. He could feel himself spinning and swirling into a sudden darkness. After a dizzying fall, he finally landed on a hard bed of stones and marbles. Dazed and confused, he dusted off his ragged body and struggled to open his eyes. He rubbed them until they opened without burning. Calvin found himself on a small, round stage, high above a crowd of cats. They had strange, bizarre faces, some squashed, others stretched, some with big, popping eyes, and others with enormous, gaping mouths and sharp teeth. The weird faces below him howled with laughter, bellowing and swaying though in slow motion and without a single sound. All Calvin could hear was the faint sound of a muffled hum echoing from deep within his head. His body wanted to scream, but all it could do was sway and bob alone on that random, solitary stage. Calvin began to sweat and quickly became slick as a frog. He raised his paw to wipe his face, and as he reached up, he felt something atop his head. It was a hat, not just any hat, but a Viking hat complete with two large horns and a shiny, metal dome. When Calvin looked down, he saw the sparkling gown that draped over his frail body like a soft tablecloth. Behind him, and in every direction, was darkness, aside from the pocket of roaring cats below that seemed to float in mid air. Suddenly, a large banner drifted above the crowd, sending

Chapter Fourteen

them into a tremendous barrage of whistles and applause. Calvin squinted his eyes and read the waving, yellow sign. Its huge brown letters said: 'TONIGHT ONLY, CALVIN THE GREAT PERFORMING HIS AWARD WINNING ONE CAT THEATER SPECTACULAR!' Calvin froze and immediately went into a panic. He couldn't remember how he got there or where he was or any of his lines. Charmed by the banner, he began to bow to his fans. Their cries slowly began to take sound, and he could soon hear every last clap and screeching howl. He stepped into a spotlight of glittery dust and took in a hearty breath. A smug grin slapped across his face. Different cats in the audience held up large posters of Calvin in an array of magical, fanciful costumes with titles of various stage productions like 'Calvin and Juliet', 'Calvin on a Hot Tin Roof', and 'Calvin and the Giant Peach'. Calvin cleared his throat and prepared himself for his monologue, when suddenly Theodore the Third from the original Slimy Cat Snacks ad came busting on stage. He slid across the wooden platform as if on wheels. The crowd threw handfuls of confetti. Theodore plowed into Calvin sending his precious Viking hat sailing above the audience, finally floating down to a clown-faced cat in the back row. Calvin tried to ignore Theodore, savoring his stage moments, when all of a sudden Theodore blurted out, "Calvin! Wake up! Wake up!" Only it wasn't Theodore's voice. Calvin didn't know who it belonged to, though it was familiar just the same. Then, to make things more confusing, a different, sweeter voice came through Theodore's screaming,

Life Two

"Come on, Calvin! Get up!" Calvin's head began to throb. "Get up, Calvin! Now!" Calvin's eyes shot open, and he shook his head. When he did, he found the familiar faces of Romeo and Tabitha peering down at him with pained expressions.

"Get up, Calvin!" Tabitha whined.

Calvin grunted and struggled to make sense of what had just happened. "Get away!" he barked, kicking Tabitha down with his hind leg. "They're waiting for me to begin! I am a star!" He wobbled to stand up, holding his head high with conceit.

"What are you talking about, Calvin?" Romeo asked. "You're not a star. Those berries drugged you."

"Can't you see?" Calvin continued. "They are here for me, Calvin the Great!" He waved his paw in front of him and bowed like a well-seasoned stage actor.

Tabitha looked at him as if he were insane. "Who?" She asked. "Calvin, *who*'s waiting for you?"

Romeo turned to Twitch, who throughout the ordeal successfully pulled and tugged his leg out of the mud. Unfortunately, as he did, he pulled with such force his body went one way and his can-opener leg the other. His body flung into a bush as his leg flew the opposite direction into another, deeper mud puddle. His muscles fluttered and flinched in the prickly branches of the bush. "What's happening to Calvin, Twitch?" Romeo blundered. "Is he dying? He

211

can't! He just can't die!"

Just then, Mr. Shadow lifted his bird-splattered head and grumbled, "Calvin, you're hallucinating! Snap out of it, boy!"

"Wha...what's happening?" Calvin mumbled, his eyes coming back into focus.

"Oh, thank goodness," Tabitha sighed. "Calvin, you're back!"

"Who are you?" Calvin yelped. "What do you want?"

Tabitha stared Calvin in the face with a look of pure confusion. "I'm Tabitha, Calvin," she uttered. "Don't you know me?"

"Don't worry about him," Twitch's voice echoed from the bush. "Give him some time. He'll be all right. He's just still a little loopy from the flower petals. He'll come around after a good night's sleep."

"He'd better!" Mr. Shadow snapped.

"We're going to need him around here," Romeo said. "There's food to find, supplies to gather, and besides, he just *better* be all right. The last thing I need around here is a cat who acts like he's on the nip!"

"How do you know about the nip?" Mr. Shadow questioned.

"Queen Elizabeth told me," he answered bashfully. "She said it's really bad stuff."

Calvin struggled up. His ordeal left his body queasy and weak. His stomach hurt something awful, and his head was spinning in circles.

Life Two

"Sit down, Calvin," Romeo urged. "You'll hurt yourself. You've been through a lot." He gently led Calvin back down to the ground.

Calvin looked up at him and began to sing in a high-pitched, horribly loud voice. "Calvin, Calvin, Calvin the Great! Calvin, Calvin..." Luckily for the others, mid-song he flopped his head back in the dirt and nodded off to sleep. However, the appalling sounds of his snoring were not anymore soothing than his horrendous singing.

Romeo gave him a quick once over to make sure he was okay. After a careful glance, he said with assurance, "Yep, he's just passed out again."

"Good," Tabitha sighed. Before she began her next sentence, she noticed Romeo running toward the water. He stopped and perched himself high atop a large stone. From there, he had an incredible view of the city. Tabitha watched for a moment then followed him. He sat alone with his head dropped low and his tail curled under his body, clutching it as if it were a doll he never, ever wanted to let go of. The bitter wind blew his fur around in circles, and small drops of sea water escaped the ravenous, crashing waves to hit him on the head.

"Romeo?" Tabitha whispered from behind. "Romeo? Are you all right?" Romeo didn't answer. "You ran away so fast, I just--."

Romeo interrupted with a heartfelt, "I wish my family were here."

Chapter Fourteen

"Oh, you'll see Dennis again real soon, I promise," Tabitha smiled, putting her paw to Romeo's shoulder.

Still keeping his back to her, Romeo said, "No, not Dennis. My family, my *real* family."

"I don't understand."

Romeo huffed and turned to face Tabitha. "You know, my mother and father and all my brothers."

"Oh," Tabitha said.

"I bet *they'd* know what to do," Romeo cried. "I bet they could help us, I mean, that was just too close. I thought we were losing Calvin forever!"

"Me too," Tabitha agreed softly. "But we didn't lose him. He's all right because *you* found the flowers. You're a good leader, Romeo." Romeo looked at her with a thank you in his eyes. "I know how scary it was. I was really scared too," Tabitha continued. "And I wish you could see your parents and brothers, but they're gone, Romeo. Hey, you know what I think?"

"What?" Romeo asked.

"I think you have their strength inside of you." She pointed to his chest. "And don't think for one minute that you aren't with your family. *We're* the best family you could ever ask for. Even Fluffy will come around, you'll see."

Romeo smiled and threw his front paws around Tabitha. They stayed like that long enough for Romeo to feel a sense of hope and belonging. Of course, she and the others were his family, the best family. All it took was a good friend to remind him.

Chapter Fifteen

Back in the coldest reaches of the city, young Dennis Crumb dashed from block to block in a desperate search for his lost cat. Under a thick sweat, he zigzagged through the streets for hours, dodging taxis and buses and loud angry horns. He zoomed passed Zaydie's Baked Ham-erie, the honey baked scent whirling through the open air. He zipped through the Crowman Elementary school yard, flinging sand and screaming, "Romeo! Romeo!"

He dashed over the security gate and back into the streets. Six blocks later he wandered into a less than safe part of the city. The buildings and its people got older, and a multitude of broken lights darkened the streets. "Romeo!" he continued to yell forcefully. Then, Dennis heard a tiny meow and saw a newspaper move. Believing it was Romeo he dashed up to the paper and snatched it away. Lying there on the cold ground was an Alley cat dining on a bird's wing.

"Gross!" Dennis flinched, launching himself back to the city. He ran faster and faster, turning his head at every moving thing. Dennis saw Romeo's sweet face in every child, animal, car, and garbage pile, only to be sadly mistaken again and again and again. Growing tired, Dennis stumbled down the next few blocks, resting at street lamps and fanning his brow. He was alone. The city was getting darker, and most people had gone home. Dennis' eyes were blurry and red and tired from their search. He propped himself up against a mailbox and looked out at the enormous city before him. It didn't like him. He could feel it in the chill up his back. With nowhere left to turn, Dennis picked up his throbbing feet and headed home.

"Just twenty dollars?" he argued with his father later that night. "I'll pay you back, pop. I swear!"

"There will be no swearing in this house!" Mr. Crumb said unfairly, crunching into a piece of beef jerky. "And if I happened to have twenty dollars laying around, I certainly wouldn't give it to some stranger just for finding your cat!"

Dennis sank to the floor and wallowed. Mr. Crumb saw the intense hurt and disappointment on his son's face.

"Look, Dennis," he said softer. "I know you miss Romeo. I miss him too." He looked at his wife who rolled her eyes. She scrunched her bottom lip

Life Two

and mouthed something of a warning. "As I was saying, Dennis," his father continued, clearing his throat. "We all want Romeo to come home, but times are tough, and I just don't have any reward money to offer. Sorry."

Dennis dropped his head and kicked Romeo's water bowl.

"Now, if you want to continue to look around the city, that's fine," Mr. Crumb said. "I'll even help you. But, there will come a time when you'll have to accept the possibility that Romeo's never coming back."

"He will!" Dennis hollered. "He will come home! You'll see! Romeo will come back!"

Mrs. Crumb put down her raw chicken breast and grabbed her son by the shoulders. "Calm down, Dennis. I've never seen you like this. Relax!"

"No!" Dennis stabbed, backing out of the kitchen. "I'm not going to relax! I'm going to find my cat, and that's that!"

Dennis trembled, his eyes filling with tears. He ran into his bedroom and flung himself on the floor, crying hysterically. Beside him lay an empty bag of litter. Dennis snatched it in his arms and hung on tight.

Chapter Sixteen

Later that day Mr. Shadow was moved to a warmer location under the statue. By now his legs were so swollen they looked like two huge, hairy sausages. Calvin was still out cold. "Has anyone seen Fluffy?" Tabitha asked. "He went away so mad this morning. I sure hope he's calmed down by now."

"Oh, you know him," Romeo sighed. "I'm sure he's fine. He's probably still looking for that flower. He'll be back soon, not that I care."

Tabitha shot him a look.

But, Fluffy wasn't back soon. He wasn't back later either. In fact, he didn't return at all. By nightfall, Romeo, Tabitha, and Twitch began to worry. Romeo and Mr. Shadow organized a search. "No one wanders off alone," Romeo warned. "I don't want to lose anybody else. Remember, there's safety in numbers."

Life Two

"He's right," Mr. Shadow agreed. "I couldn't have said it better myself. Nobody, *nobody* goes off alone!" From where he lay, he waved a twig around to make his point seem more critical. It didn't work as he accidentally poked himself in the eye with it. "Twitch?" he called.

"Yes, Mr. Shadow," Twitch promptly answered.

"Can you think of anywhere, *anywhere* on this island where Fluffy might be? Is there a secret hiding place, or a cat-eating monster, or something? What about those circus trees?"

Romeo and Tabitha shuddered and held tightly to one another.

"There's all kinda weird places around here. He could be anywhere." Twitch quivered under his pink fur.

"Okay everyone, let's get on with the search. We'll check back in with Mr. Shadow in one hour," Romeo explained. "Maybe Fluffy will return here on his own."

"What should I do with *him*?" Mr. Shadow asked, pointing to Calvin who lay in a puddle of his own urine.

"Just leave him be," Twitch said. "He's wasted. He'll sleep like a baby for a while yet."

Throughout the better part of the night, the three cats searched and searched, staying clear out of sight of the deranged elephant trees. But, with nowhere left to look, Fluffy still had not been found.

"Are you *sure* there's no place he may have gone?" Romeo asked Twitch.

Twitch faced his two new friends with a touch of uneasiness. "Well, I suppose there is *one* spot we haven't looked." His eyes wandered about, and his ears began to rattle uncontrollably making awkward noises.

Tabitha stared at him puzzled. "What's going on with your head?"

Twitch put both front paws over his ears to stop the shaking. "Oh, it's nothing. This happens all the time since the lab."

"Oh," Tabitha said.

"So where's this place you're talking about?" Romeo asked.

"What place?" Twitch asked.

"The place you mentioned. Where Fluffy might be."

Twitch took a meager step back. "Oh, yeah... well, we don't want to go there tonight. Besides, if he is there, we won't be able to do anything until tomorrow, when it's daylight."

"Why?" Tabitha asked nervously. "Is it a secret cave filled with cat eating trolls or something?"

"No, of course not," Twitch muttered. "It's--."

Romeo stepped forward aggressively and got right in Twitch's face, rattling ears and all. "Tell us, Twitch! What is it?"

"It's a hole," Twitch blurted out. "I warned Fluffy

that it could be dangerous. He didn't listen, and now he's probably fallen in."

"Why didn't you tell us about this before?" Romeo huffed.

"Because--."

"Because why?" Romeo pestered.

"Because I'm scared to go back there!" Twitch wailed. "Don't make me do it! Please!"

"This is ridiculous!" Tabitha wailed. She breathed in and took a softer approach. "So, you've been in this... hole?" Twitch nodded and kicked the ground. "Tell us about it. I promise, nobody will be mad at you." She nudged Romeo, who still had a foul grimace on his face.

"Uh...yeah, sorry, Twitch. I won't yell. Promise." Romeo said.

Romeo and Tabitha sat down to listen to Twitch's story. "Some say," he began, "that the hole is haunted!"

"Haunted?" Romeo asked.

"Haunted by what?" Tabitha shivered.

"Haunted by the spirits of the dead pirates. Supposedly, long ago before the statue and the city, a great pirate ship headed for the mainland. It had huge black, swinging flags and filthy, peg-legged men with stinky breath and dirty patches over their eyes. They were in search of rich treasures and hardy women. Well, legend has it that their ship struck a rock on this very island. The ship was badly damaged. After a

Chapter Sixteen

few hours, it sunk. The pirates were marooned on the island. Some of them ate each other to stay alive. One day a big storm erupted and flung the survivors into the sea to their deaths. One by one they plunged into the dark waters, all the way down to the very ship they came on. Dead, every last one of them! As their revenge, many believe they still haunt this island, particularly the large hole they created to hide the jewels they salvaged from their sinking ship before it went down. The jewels are gone, taken by some people who found them when the statue was built, but the ghosts of the pirates still search for their treasure. I walked by it once, and I swear I heard moaning coming from deep in the ground! So, as you can plainly see, I am terrified of that hole!"

Romeo and Tabitha sat motionless, their eyes as wide as the moon. Finally, Romeo spoke. "That's the most ridiculous story I've ever heard. There are no pirates! And there are no ghosts either!" Romeo folded his paws over his chest and shook his head. "Take me there! Now!"

"He was right about the elephant trees," Tabitha whispered in Romeo's ear.

"I know, and I don't care," Romeo said. "Take us there, Twitch!"

"No!" Twitch begged. "I swear! It's true! The pirates! An old rat told me. He and his entire family saw them. The story was passed down from generation to generation. It's true!"

Life Two

"Yeah?" Romeo asked. "So, where is this rat now?"

"He's dead. His whole family died in last year's snowstorm. They didn't hide fast enough. Okay, so maybe I ate them a little. I was hungry, all right?"

"Maybe it's all true," Tabitha trembled. "What if the rat was right? I'm frightened. This sounds a lot more scary than the elephant trees," she said, as if she had already forgotten about her recent death.

"You don't like Fluffy anymore, remember?" Twitch whined.

"Don't be silly, besides we haven't got any other choice," Romeo urged. "If Fluffy is in that *hole*, we'll be sure to find him and get him out. But I can assure you, there are no ghosts!"

By now it had gotten quite cold, and the clouds looked angry. They were thick and the color of rain, and seemed to be closing in over the island. They were low, so low in fact that the head of the great statue had disappeared into the misty mess behind the faded moonlight. Mr. Shadow looked up and wondered if she was still there, hiding somewhere in the clouds. He imagined them parting and seeing his head resting atop the enormous stone body.

After a quick and tense jaunt, the cats reached the forbidden hole. It was hidden behind a bathroom building. Everyone pinched their noses and walked by. "There it is," Twitch pointed. "I'll just wait back here. You guys can go ahead."

Chapter Sixteen

Romeo rolled his eyes and carefully walked up. An array of pretty flowers lay just at the rim, and an odd mist seeped from the ground. Tabitha stood behind Romeo, trying hard not to think of the murderous pirates. She wondered how they all had one missing eye. Was it just coincidence? Or was it some morbid pirate ritual? And what about those peg legs?

Slowly, Romeo peered ever-so-subtly into the hole. At first he saw nothing, only darkness. Then he stuck his nose in deeper. Suddenly he slipped on a pretty yellow flower, nearly falling in. Tabitha gasped in fear.

"Fluffy?" Romeo called, scrambling to his feet. "Fluffy? Are you in there?" No answer, just the faint sounds of a far off chorus of crickets. "Fluffy?" he tried again. "Can you hear me? It's Romeo! I'm sorry about our fight! You're my best friend, and I..."

Just then, Tabitha walked up, peeked over Romeo's shoulder and said, "Come on, Romeo. He's obviously not in there. You did all you could do. Perhaps he fell into the water and is floating around somewhere."

All of a sudden, a low moan echoed from deep within the hole. Romeo grabbed the ground with his two front paws and stuck his little head in as far as he possibly could. "Fluffy? Fluffy?" This time the moan got louder. Romeo recognized that sound right away. It was Fluffy. "That's him! That's him! Good work, Twitch." Tabitha and Romeo began to dance around like two little kids on Halloween with a bag full of caramel.

"Are you sure that wasn't a pirate ghost you heard down there?" Twitch quivered.

"Naw," Romeo said. "That's Fluffy. I just know it. Now get over here. There are no pirates down there." Romeo could sense the enormity of the hole in the way his voice echoed and bounced its way down to Fluffy. It was very deep and very narrow. Getting Fluffy out of there unharmed would be a definite challenge.

Tabitha looked over the spot as well. "What do we do now, Romeo?" she asked. "How do we get him out?"

Everyone paced back and forth and concentrated hard. Fluffy's moans below sounded deeper and more riddled with pain. Something drastic had to be done and fast!

"I've got it!" Romeo shouted.

Everyone lit up.

"Twitch," Romeo said. "Do you have a box and some string?"

"Uh, yeah. Why?"

"Let's get it. I'll tell you later."

"What is it, Romeo?" Tabitha asked bright eyed. "What are you going to do?"

"Later, Tab, later." Romeo ran off before turning back to her. "Tabitha, you stay here and keep an eye on that hole. If you hear any 'Ahoy, Matees,' come find us quick."

Chapter Sixteen

Twitch's ears twitched furiously.

Tabitha nodded as Romeo ran off with Twitch. He took Romeo to the back of the visitor's building and through a long vent that led them down an endless hallway. Near a turn in the vent, Twitch lifted up a small, rusted lever that led to another vent going down into the basement. The two cats had to jump into that vent to reach their destination. "Hold on tight, and look straight ahead!" Twitch hollered as they slid down the metal walls. Romeo shut his eyes tightly and curled himself into a ball. Then, with a loud thump the two cats landed on a large pile of old newspapers. "Here we are," Twitch announced. "Come on!"

Romeo was still in his huddle with his eyelids closed tight. Twitch nudged him in the leg.

"Where are we?" Romeo asked, opening his eyes slowly.

"My home," Twitch said untangling his two tails. "This is where I live." He held out his paw and led Romeo to his own private, tucked away world. It was a fairly large space between the vent and the actual wall leading into the basement where the people came. The place was certainly a dump. It smelled putrid and felt damp and musty, making Romeo gag. The place was lined with soiled newspapers, old, moldy sweatshirts and jackets, stinky shoes, and mounds of insect exoskeletons. Though not appealing whatsoever, it was cozy in its own awkward way. Romeo noticed a large stuffed doll resembling the statue on which Twitch slept each night. The face was covered with a foreign yellow stain. There were strange little plants lining the walls all neatly planted into used popcorn tubs and lost baseball caps. Though most of them were dead, Twitch kept them around as company just the same.

"You live *here*?" Romeo asked half in awe, half in disgust.

"I've been here since I came to the island," Twitch admitted. "I like it. It's a lot better than that awful cage I was living in at the lab. Nobody bothers me down here, and it even stays pretty warm. I bring things down that the tourists leave behind. There's always tons of stuff. I guess they don't do a very good job of cleaning up the place."

"Yeah, I guess not." Romeo said eying the mountain of fur balls in the corner. "Don't you ever get lonely?"

Twitch nervously fluffed one of his dead plants to ease his discomfort over Romeo's question. "Uh, naw...not really," he lied. "Like I said, I like it."

"So Twitch?" Romeo asked. "Where are the box and the string?"

"Easy, let me show you." Twitch showed Romeo a small box that he found in a garbage can outside. It was hidden behind a large beam. Twitch pushed it out. He looked inside and quickly tossed out three banana peels when Romeo wasn't looking. "I figured I may need this some day, so I took it." He went on to fetch some string, of which he had plenty. "What are you going to do with it, Romeo?" Twitch asked eagerly.

"Simple," Romeo said with suavity. "I'm going to lower the box into the hole with the string so we can put Fluffy inside. Then we can raise him up. What do you think?"

"Awesome!" Twitch said impressed. "How'd you ever think of that?"

"Survival class," Romeo bragged. "Mr. Shadow is a genius. He taught us all kinds of cool stuff like that just in case we ever got into a jam. I never actually thought I'd have to use any of it though."

"Wow, survival class," Twitch glowed. "Who's going to go down in the box to find him? You or Tabitha?"

"How about you?"

Twitch's ears began to rattle out of control, and his nose flared. "N...n...no, I...I...couldn't. The pirates!"

"Oh, don't be silly," Romeo teased. "Beside, maybe you'll find some buried treasure down there. After all, that's where they hid it, didn't they?"

"Whatever," Twitch trembled. "Let's just take the string and the box and get out of here."

Twitch showed Romeo how to get out of the building through another vent at the opposite side of his home. It led up and outside. Though it was tricky crawling at that angle, they managed, even with all their equipment. Soon they were back with Tabitha at the hole explaining the entire plan. She agreed it was

Life Two

worth a try, and being the smallest she would be the one lowered into the ground. Relieved, Twitch cut the string with his walrus tooth and punctured two holes in the box with his real can-opener leg.

"I don't know about this, Romeo," Tabitha admitted. "I mean, what if there really are pirates down there? You said yourself you heard moaning."

Romeo nuzzled up next to her and looked her straight in the eyes. "Tabitha," he said, "You've got to do this for Fluffy. Now, if anyone can do this, it's you! You've stood up to Fidel, you've escaped from the Pound, and now you're going to save Fluffy. I trust you, and I'm going to be right here. Just tug on the string if there is any problem."

She nodded.

Once the string was attached by way of the holes, Tabitha climbed in the box and was lowered by Twitch and Romeo. Romeo watched her go down, down, down. Twitch kept his head completely turned away with the most frightened, shriveled expression on his face. "No pirates, no pirates, no pirates," he whispered over and over. "No pirates, no pirates..."

Finally, a soft voice echoed from below. "I'm at the bottom!" It was Tabitha. She had made it.

"Do you see Fluffy?" Romeo asked excited.

There was a long pause then Tabitha finally shouted back, "It's super dark down here! I can hardly see a thing! And boy does it smell!"

"Do you see Fluffy?" Romeo called louder.

Chapter Sixteen

"Ask her if she sees any pirates?" Twitch whispered.

Romeo glared at him. "No."

"Ahh!" Tabitha suddenly screamed.

"What is it?" Romeo demanded.

No answer.

"Tab?" he yelled again. "What's wrong?"

"One of those big, yucky spiders just fell from the ceiling. I don't know where it went!" she shouted up, her voice echoing off the dirt walls.

"Just find Fluffy, and we'll pull you guys outta there!"

"Eeek!" Tabitha screeched. "It just walked across my paw! Get me up! Get me up!"

"No! Find Fluffy, and forget the darn spider! Are you a cat or a coward?"

"A coward!" Tabitha wept. Twitch and Romeo could hear her sobbing below. They heard a loud thump then a hiss.

"What the heck is going on down there? Do you see Fluffy or not?"

"Yes, he's out cold and the spider's right in front of him!" Tabitha wailed.

"Yikes!" Twitch gasped."

"I'm throwing rocks at him, but he won't move!"

"Be careful, Tabitha. The spider could kill you both!" Twitch warned then turned to Romeo. "I'm serious. I've seen it."

Romeo squinted his eyes and thought hard.

Life Two

"Cover it with dirt and grab Fluffy real fast! You can do it, Tabitha!"

"Nooo," she wailed. "I'm afraid!"

"Tabitha!" Romeo hollered. "Now!"

Deep in the hole, Tabitha's entire body shook. She reached down and positioned her paw next to a tiny hill of dirt, keeping one eye on the arachnid. With a swat she sent the dirt flying toward the spider. It wiggled and moved on its eight creepy legs as Tabitha frantically kicked more and more dirt on top of it until it was completely covered. She ran over to Fluffy and pulled and tugged with all her might. She yanked him over to the box as one tiny spider leg sprouted from the dirt, then another and another.

"Hurry!" Romeo echoed above.

Tabitha tried, but she couldn't get Fluffy into that box. By now the entire spider sat atop the dirt mound staring at her viciously. Tabitha got an idea. She quickly put the box on its side and rolled Fluffy in. She flung herself repeatedly into the box hoping to knock it on its bottom with her and Fluffy inside. It didn't work. She had to give herself a running start, but that meant getting near the spider, for it was coming her way. Tabitha grabbed the edge of the box with her teeth and turned it around so it faced the other direction. She took several steps back for her run.

"Ouch!" She tripped. Below her paw was a shiny object, like gold. In an instant she snatched it with her teeth and charged for the box just as one ugly spider

Chapter Sixteen

leg began to creep up the side. Flop! The box fell on its bottom with Tabitha and Fluffy safely inside. The spider was nowhere in sight. Tabitha dropped the shiny find beside Fluffy. "Pull us up, Romeo! Fast!" she yelled.

Romeo and Twitch tugged at the strings until Tabitha had finally made it to the top. The box wobbled out of the hole and again fell on its side.

"Fluffy!" Romeo shouted.

"Wow!" Tabitha said, her heart pounding. "That was scary but I guess all those stamina workouts paid off."

"Um...um...um!" Twitch shook with a dazed expression pointing to the box.

"What is it, Twitch?" Romeo asked.

"Sp-spider!" Twitch howled.

Sure enough, the spider was clinging to the underside of the box. Everyone screamed and scrambled to get away. Poor Fluffy still lay inside. One of the eight legs touched the ground. Romeo inched up slowly.

"Stay away from it, Romeo," Tabitha warned. "Remember what Twitch said!"

But Romeo continued on, coming face to face with the dangerous bug. "Come on over, guys. He's dead." Romeo showed everyone the dead carcass of the crushed spider. Green slop oozed out from all angles.

"I probably crushed him when I flew into the box. He must have been under it."

"Lucky for you," Romeo said.

Tabitha breathed a sigh of relief.

Life Two

She and Romeo were happy to see Fluffy alive and moaning. Romeo kicked the spider remains off the box and began dragging it back toward the statue. Fluffy's sleepy head bounced against the sides. The sky began to drizzle, making the ground thicker and harder to walk on.

As they trudged, Romeo noticed a strange clinking noise. "Is that you?" Romeo asked Twitch. "I hear something."

Twitch glanced around at all his oddities. "Nope, not me."

"It must be this," Tabitha said grabbing the shiny thing from the box. It was a medallion attached to a long, gold chain. She put it around her neck. "I forgot. I found this in the hole."

Twitch dropped the strings and stared. "Wow," Twitch said with a sigh. "Pirates!"

"You just found that?" Romeo asked.

"Yeah," Tabitha said. "Maybe it's lost treasure after all."

"Ugh," Twitch yelped.

"Look, there's writing on it." Romeo noticed.

Tabitha held it up in the light as she wiggled it around in her paw. She squinted at the big, jaggedly, carved words. "I think it says, *Life is a treasure.*" She stared at it closely to make sure. "Yep. Life is a treasure."

"What does that mean?" Romeo wondered.

"Got me," Tabitha said. "Mushy stuff, I guess."

Twitch scratched his human nose and said

without fear, "Wow, pirates."

All four cats soon made it back to Mr. Shadow. When they reached him, he had an irritated look and was screaming something about Calvin. "He thinks he's a gorilla!" Mr. Shadow hollered to the others. "Get him away from me!"

Calvin was standing on three paws with his butt sticking out. Using his fourth paw he picked at his behind and stuffed little morsels into his mouth. He circled Mr. Shadow and made loud gorilla noises. Romeo walked up to him with a curious grin. "Calvin?" he asked. "Calvin, are you all right?"

"Oo-oo-oo," Calvin bellowed.

"It's that berry he ate," Twitch announced. "It's still in his system. It's going to take more time."

Mr. Shadow knocked Calvin's butt out of his face and angrily asked, "How much more time? He's driving me crazy! I've got to get some sleep!"

"At least he doesn't think he's Calvin the Great any longer," Tabitha offered. "We get enough of that attitude back home."

"Quickly!" Mr. Shadow screamed. "Scratch my leg!" I've got a bite that's killing me!"

Romeo, Tabitha, and Twitch all lunged for Mr. Shadow's itchy leg. They dove head first, all piling on top of his broken bones. Mr. Shadow let out a howl that could awaken the dead.

Over the next hour Tabitha, Twitch, and Romeo told Mr. Shadow about their exciting adventure into

Life Two

the secret pirate cave and of Tabitha's golden medallion. Fluffy was taken out of the box and placed on a warm spot near Mr. Shadow. Mr. Shadow carefully inspected his body as best he could. He specifically checked for bumps and other injuries. "You say he fell down a long, rocky hole?" The others nodded. "And he doesn't have one scratch?" he asked again.

"What are you getting at, Mr. Shadow?" Romeo asked.

Mr. Shadow looked up at the others with sad eyes. "Well," he began. "There's no possible way he would have fallen so far and sustained no injuries. He must have had at least one. Since everything's all healed up, it could only mean that he--."

"Lost a life?" Tabitha blurted. "Oh, my, Fluffy lost a life! He must have! I was in that hole, and I have lots of scratches. And I didn't even fall! Surely he would have cut himself!"

"I can't take this place anymore!" Romeo belted out. "I hate it! Oh, Fluffy!"

"He's going to be all right, Romeo," Tabitha said warmly. "We saved him. He's back. Remember what Queen Elizabeth said, 'losing a life is *part* of life.' That's just the way it is."

"Yeah?" Romeo snapped. "And where is she now? Huh? She's dead! She left me! Why couldn't she be here now? We need her!" Romeo turned away and ran off. This time Tabitha let him be.

235

Chapter Seventeen

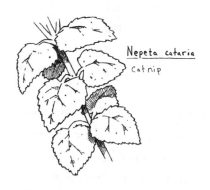

Nepeta cataria
Catnip

Deep in the city, a romping ruckus from the Glitteroom burst from the pipes and filled the alley as its faithful patrons enjoyed beer after beer. The brew mugs clinked, and the Alley mugs grinned. A cloud of laughter and a shower of whistles dangled above the chairs and tables. On the tiny stage paraded a bevy of performers, classier than the ones at Kitty's Cabaret, the usual spot, but seedy enough just the same. Raven dazzled everyone as she slinked across a beam singing her heart out. As always, Fidel sat at his table, the best table, and slowly sank into his little world of fantasy.

"More! More!" he cheered. "Do it again!"

In and around the tables, waitresses zigzagged with trays filled with beer mugs and roaches. Sissy, one of the new girls, spilled a mug on Max, the boss of the joint.

Life Two

"Don't worry about it, toots," he said. "We'll deal with this later." He gave her a wink and shooed her away. Sissy felt a shiver run up her back and went back to her tables.

Alongside Fidel and Max sat Clink, Mustard, Honey, Cheeseburger, and Jailbird. This table was the drunkest in the club and the loudest. They carried on like a fraternity of wackos, pinching the waitresses and jumping on the chairs. Fidel made certain his newest gang member, Jailbird, had a most memorable time. He continued feeding him pockets of nip and shoved drink after drink into his ratty face. Jailbird slouched in his chair, the room spinning around him. His eyes were stuck wide open though his insides were collapsing from an exhausting week of heavy partying. He drooled on the table until his head finally plopped down into his thimble of beer. Cheeseburger pounded to the beat of the music from the club above, causing Jailbird's head to slap up and down against the wooden table.

"Get up!" Fidel screamed. "What are you doing?" He lifted Jailbird's head by his ears and stared at his face. "You look fine," Fidel barked. "You just need some more nip. That'll wake you up." Fidel looked around the bar. "Bait!" he called, spotting his crony. Bait wasn't allowed to sit at Fidel's table. He was in trouble for popping a huge bunch of balloons in the city at a little girl's birthday party. It caused a horrible commotion, and the Pound came and picked

Chapter Seventeen

up two innocent Alleys, although nobody of particular importance to Fidel. *Weaklings*, he had said. "Bait! Get our friend here some more nip and another beer. Make it a strong one." He winked at Bait and gave Jailbird a friendly smack on the back.

Bait returned with the concoction. "Jailbird, open wide!" Bait grabbed Jailbird by the chin and nose and pried open his mouth. Jailbird, with his wired eyes, resisted and shook his head no. Fidel glared in his direction. Jailbird reluctantly opened his mouth for Bait. His tongue quivered and trembled as the stinging nip slid down his throat once more. When it was all over and the catnip began to work its spell, he smiled at Fidel and sipped some beer. His expression immediately changed. His head perked up, and he said in a poised and easy manner, "You really know how to party, Fidel."

With that, the spirits grew higher, the females shimmied wilder, and the Alleys drank till morning.

Chapter Eighteen

The next few days on the island were dreadful. The rain had left the ground soggy and impossible to walk on. Sick and hopeless, the six cats spent the days alone wandering from bench to bench, thinking of their people. It didn't take much to get them angry at each other. Tempers were short, and their silences were long. Twinkle Toes' name was hardly mentioned anymore. They all were too busy thinking about themselves and their desperate situation.

Fluffy awoke from his traumatic experience dazed and bewildered at the loss of a life, however, he resumed arguing and bickering with Romeo. Twitch continued to help when necessary, though he spent much of his time huddled in his tiny crawl space. Mr. Shadow lay in the same, tiresome spot eating his paltry meals with the help of Tabitha. And Calvin went from believing he was Julius Caesar to an angry herd of water buffalo, and finally to a mad swarm of killer bees. He buzzed around all day stinging the others with his claw.

Everyone finally agreed to go see Romeo's shark. Despite their attempts to drag it on shore to eat, it was just far too big and heavy to do so.

The days were growing shorter, and hope was dwindling fast.

One crisp and lonely night, Romeo felt particularly low. While everyone slept soundly, he decided in an irrational moment to travel to the highest point of the beautiful statue and jump from her sculpted hair to his ultimate death. He would plummet down the statue's body and allow the cool air to flow through him. If he was still alive when he *hopefully* hit the water, as he sank he would choke until each of his eight remaining lives were sucked out of him one by one. Fluffy was right. Everything bad that had happened to the Sticks was because of him. They would be better off if he was gone. He would finally give Fidel what he wanted. Once he was completely and forever out of the picture, there would be no more problems between the Sticks and the Alleys.

"Nobody will care," he muttered to himself. The rest of his friends could go home and inform Fidel that Romeo was gone for good. Dead all nine times. The fighting would stop. Peace would return to the city. He felt most sorry for Tabitha. Surely she would be upset with him, but it would pass. He was too delusional at the time to think otherwise.

Before he pressed the elevator button, Romeo took a long, last look at his friends sleeping nearby. Regardless of all the tragedy and hardship they experienced in the past week, they somehow looked peaceful and calm. But not Romeo, inside he was a mass of nerves, jumbled emotions, and delirious thoughts. He even tried to eat one of the berries Calvin ate just to feel different for a day. He held the juicy berry over his mouth for an entire ten minutes, only to put it down after he remembered seeing Calvin throw up seven times in a row from the effects. But now, there he stood winking his final goodbyes to those he loved the most.

As quietly as he could, he called the elevator and stepped into the big metal box. Up he went, above the island, above the water, and out of his senses.

When the big doors opened, he stepped out and crawled to the highest point on the statue he could reach. From there, the city was even smaller and prettier than ever. When he squinted his eyes, he could almost see Dennis' building. Oh, how he ached for poor Dennis. Romeo figured after a week apart though, Dennis had probably gotten a new kitten and forgotten all about his beloved Romeo.

From where he stood, Romeo closed his eyes and allowed himself to feel nature's wind whirl through his fur and dab tiny raindrops on his face. His paws

Chapter Eighteen

were holding tightly to the stone lady, grinding little dust particles off as he shuddered. Looking down, he could see the water far, far below. To reach it he knew he must leap as hard and as far out as he could or he'd miss and splatter on the ground. He couldn't do that to Tabitha. It would be too much for her to bear. So, he took in a heavy breath, closed his eyes tightly, and prepared himself for his final jump.

Suddenly, a vicious gust of wind pushed him backwards on his bottom. Stunned, he shook his head back and forth and attempted to stand up again. Then something caught his eye. It was the very wind that knocked him over. To his surprise, it began to take shape. Romeo backed away on his butt using his back paws to guide him, when two sharp, purple dots began to glow at the center of the cloud. They looked like eyes. As Romeo concentrated and focused, he saw Queen Elizabeth. She floated before him in an almost ghostly display of mystery and wonder. Romeo rubbed his eyes over and over but only saw more clearly her striking image hovering in front of him. Could it be true? Could it really be her? Surely, he must be dreaming. Scared, he reached out a paw to touch her. It passed right through her.

"Yes, it's me, Romeo," Queen Elizabeth said in a softer voice than he was used to. "I'm really here."

Speechless, Romeo stared stunned, his jaw hanging low.

"I can't stay for long," she said kindly. "But I

Life Two

do have something I need to tell you, something you need to hear."

Romeo gazed up at her in complete awe. "Q-Queen Eliz-z-z-abeth?" he sputtered. "Is that r-r-really you?"

She smiled as she floated against the faded stars. "Yes. Now, Romeo, what are you doing? Why are you up here?"

Romeo struggled for something to say. He wiggled his paws around and kept pointing to the water. "I-I couldn't sleep."

"A lie!" Queen Elizabeth scolded. "You were going to jump! You were going to end your lives just when your friends need you the most! I want you to listen, Romeo, and I want you to listen good." She drifted closer to him, chilling him even more. "When I lost my ninth life, I knew I was too young to die. I had so much I wanted to do, so much I wanted to see. You still can, Romeo. You're a baby. You have years ahead of you and people and friends who love you. We're not ready for you up here. If you jump, you'll never have peace within yourself. I thought you were stronger than this, Romeo. At least your *parents* thought you were! Now get down from this statue and take your friends off this island. Go back to the Factory and make things right. Stop Fidel before he kills again. And remember, *nothing* is your fault! It's up to you, Romeo. They all need you. They all need you..." As she repeated those four words over and

Chapter Eighteen

over, her voice began to fade and the cloud she created swirled once again into a fearless wind and flew away into nowhere.

Off in the far away distance, Romeo spotted a fishing boat sitting alone in the harbor. As if a light bulb lit over his head, he jumped back into the elevator and soared down to the bottom level. He raced out as soon as the doors cracked open and woke Mr. Shadow and the others. "Wake up! Wake up!" he screamed, shaking them out of their slumber.

Mr. Shadow cleared his scratchy throat. "What's going on here?" he mumbled. "Romeo? What are you doing?"

"I've got it! I've got it!" Romeo wailed.

"All you've got is a case of the weirds!" Tabitha snapped groggily.

"I know how to get out of here! We'll build a boat!" Romeo yelled jumping up and down.

"What's gotten into you?" Mr. Shadow said sitting up out of his sleep. "A boat? Have you lost your mind?"

"Maybe!" Romeo beamed.

"It's the middle of the night, and you need to get some sleep!" Mr. Shadow growled. "Now shut your eyes, and we'll discuss this silly idea in the morning! *In the morning!*"

Romeo smiled and put his head down. His mind was racing with unreal thoughts of Queen Elizabeth and his incredible experience on the statue. He was too pumped to sleep, filled with thoughts of home and Dennis and his other Stick friends at the Factory.

The next morning everyone awoke to find Romeo missing. It was very early, and he was not in his usual sleeping spot. Worried, the others began to panic. "Where could he be?" Tabitha asked in a frenzy. "I can't go through *this* again!"

"Maybe he's still mad at me," Fluffy suggested.

"Nonsense!" Mr. Shadow said, having no memory of the boat conversation. "I'm sure he's here somewhere. Why don't you split up and look for him? Maybe he found some tasty fish for breakfast."

Tabitha, Fluffy, and Calvin had just started to walk away when Twitch and Romeo walked up.

"Hey, everybody!" Twitch said.

"Romeo, where have you been?" Tabitha asked.

"I couldn't sleep, so I went to see Twitch about my boat idea," he boasted.

"Boat?" Mr. Shadow interrupted. "What boat? We can't build a boat. That's ludicrous. We can hardly kill a spider."

"Maybe not a boat, but we can surely build a raft!" Twitch said bright eyed.

"A raft?" everyone asked at once.

"Yes, it's so obvious," Twitch explained. "I've got a ton of wood and string at my place. We can tie it all together, and you guys can sail out of here!"

Chapter Eighteen

"You, too, Twitch," Tabitha reminded him.

Twitch didn't say anything.

Mr. Shadow began rubbing his chin, a clear sign he was deep in thought. "You know," he said. "It just might work. Anyway, I sure think it's worth a try!"

"Let's do it!" they all cheered.

For the rest of the day, the cats helped in building the raft, except for Calvin. He was busy slithering around like a snake trying to shed his skin. He writhed in the mud making everyone sick. Fluffy was still weak from his unfortunate death and spent much of the time sitting with Mr. Shadow planning the final escape. Twitch and Romeo brought up some wooden planks from the building's basement along with gobs of string. Tabitha was practicing knots and teaching herself the best ways to connect all the wood together. By mid-afternoon as the fish and birds and flies took their daily naps, Tabitha, Romeo, and Twitch almost had the raft complete. It stretched six planks wide, roughly five feet in length. The thick twine wrapped tightly around and in between each splintery board holding the entire raft together. Romeo, Twitch, and Tabitha stood back a moment and marveled at their accomplishment.

"Is it going to work?" Mr. Shadow asked the little engineers.

"Well, it should," Tabitha said proudly. "I tied all the knots just like you told me to."

"Let's throw her in the water and see how

she does!" Romeo said happily in this moment of triumph.

Twitch and Romeo tossed the raft into the water. Everyone stood near the edge to watch it meet the bay. Mr. Shadow sat in his box. The water was murky and topped with a few floating, rusted beer cans and sandwich bags. Calvin was finally quiet, much to everyone's joy.

"It floats! It floats!" Tabitha cried.

"We did it!" Twitch roared.

"We can finally go home!" Romeo yelled the loudest. "Even you, Twitch! You get to come home with us! Leave this dumpy island!"

Twitch stepped back into the shadow of the statue's long arm. "I don't think so, guys," he said. "I belong here. This is my home now." A bird dropping fell on his head.

"Nonsense," Mr. Shadow snapped. "You belong with us, and that's final! Now it's time to test the raft. We need a brave volunteer to see if it can hold any weight. Who will it be?"

Nobody volunteered. No one wanted to be the guinea pig. After all, what if the raft didn't work?

"What about you, Romeo?" Tabitha asked. "After all, you're our leader, aren't you?"

"Yeah, *Romeo*," Fluffy whined. "Hop on!"

Romeo nervously bit his lip. "You're right. It was my idea, so here goes."

Just then, Calvin stomped forward pushing

Chapter Eighteen

everyone aside, nose to the sky. "Let me through. Outta my way!"

"What are you doing, Calvin?" Fluffy chimed.

"Calvin? Who's Calvin? I'm General Hawkins of the Third Regiment," Calvin bragged as he saluted to everyone. "Fall out and about face, soldiers! Hup! Hup!"

"Huh?" Tabitha asked.

"He's really lost his mind this time," Romeo whispered into Tabitha's ear. "It's still those flowers."

"Step aside, let a professional handle this." Calvin marched forward like a brave soldier and took his spot near the edge of the water. Below, the lone raft bobbed and rolled to the rhythm of the waves.

"Wait, Cal...I mean, General," Mr. Shadow rang. "Make sure you get on slowly."

Too late. Calvin took a running leap and flung himself onto the raft.

"No!" Mr. Shadow screamed. "Be careful! *Careful*! I don't want that thing capsizing!"

The weight of Calvin's body rocked the planks sending tiny waves crashing up over the sides. Orange rinds and cigarette butts splashed in his face. Calvin wobbled around, catching his balance at the center of the raft. Everybody watched with gritted teeth and prayed to the Almighty Bubastis. Suddenly, as Calvin began a victory march, a large bubble sputtered up from below the raft and belched its way out of the water. Another bubble did the same, then another, and another until it was obvious the raft was sinking. Calvin continued, unaware of the dangers around him. The other cats watched, speechless, as dozens of tiny bubbles surrounded their rescue raft as if it were being pulled down like a great ship. The salty water quickly reached Calvin's toes, then his tail. "Hey!" Calvin shouted, frantically running in circles. "What's going on, here? Sergeant? Call the troops! Send in the Navy!"

"What the...? What do we..?" Fluffy rumbled.

"Get him out of there!" Romeo hollered.

The scene turned completely chaotic. Everyone scrambled around as Calvin plunged into the cold, polluted water. Helpless to the situation, Mr. Shadow struggled on the bench. "Romeo!" he called dramatically. "Get him out of there! *Now!*"

Lickety-split, Romeo and Fluffy grabbed hold of the soggy cat and pulled with all their might, each trying to out do the other. Calvin struggled and fought, believing he could take on the dangerous waters alone.

"Oh give it up, already!" Fluffy yelled angrily. But Calvin continued to flop and wiggle.

Romeo's and Fluffy's strong and agile muscles had grown weak after days of little food or sleep. Thinking fast, Twitch firmly planted his can-opener leg into the grass, scratched his human nose and lunged as far forward as he could into the water with the rest of his body. He stretched out his front paw toward

Chapter Eighteen

Calvin who was by now completely submerged and bobbing around like a speared fish. "Calvin, grab onto my paw!" Twitch roared.

"I'm not Calvin!" the General insisted, gagging on the water.

"General! Whatever!" Twitch roared. "Just grab on tight! I'll pull you out!"

Calvin gave in and paddled to Twitch's outstretched paw. He was no swimmer. With his back paws kicking violently, he extended his front paws. His head sunk immediately with one little whisker jutting out of the water.

Instinctively, Twitch pulled his leg from the mud and dove into the water. He disappeared for a scary moment, but emerged in a breath holding Calvin high above his head. With a force no cat had ever seen before, Twitch flung Calvin's soggy body out of the water and onto the ground. Panting heavily, Twitch quickly grabbed a firmly planted rock, and with the same burst of strength lifted himself out of the water and beside Calvin. Twitch's wet body immediately began to quiver and quake. Calvin didn't move a muscle. Tabitha ran over to see if the two males were all right. "Calvin! Calvin!" she screamed as she rattled his body up and down. "Calvin! Speak to me!"

"Check his pulse!" Mr. Shadow yelled. "You know, see if his heart's beating!"

Tabitha did as Mr. Shadow said. She put her ear to Calvin's chest. Sure enough, Calvin's heart was racing away. He was alive, but unconscious. Relieved, Tabitha quickly shot over to Twitch. Unlike Calvin, he was alert, though exhausted and hurt. His odd body trembled out of control. "I...I'm okay," Twitch whispered. "Help...them...with...the...raft."

Tabitha whipped her head around and saw Romeo and Fluffy peering over the edge into the water. She ran to them and looked in. "Where is it?" she asked frantically. "Where's the raft?"

Romeo gazed at her with sad eyes and shook his head. He couldn't even speak.

"It's gone," Fluffy sighed.

"Gone?" Tabitha blurted, looking at them as if they were crazy. "Well, don't just stand there! Let's jump in and get it!"

Romeo and Fluffy had no reaction.

"Fine, if you're not going in, I will!" Tabitha stood at the edge, closed her eyes, and bent her back legs about to dive in when Romeo grabbed her shoulders and held her down.

"It's gone, Tab! Sunk to the bottom! We can't get it back! It didn't work!"

"No!" she wailed. "It has to work! It has to!"

"It's all Calvin's fault!" Fluffy exploded. "He jumped on it too hard!"

"Look, Fluffy," Romeo said sternly. "It's nobody's fault! Not Calvin's, not mine, not anyone's! The sooner you realize that, the quicker we'll get home!"

"We can rebuild!" Twitch stepped in between the

arguing Sticks. "We'll just make another raft!"

"That won't work," Mr. Shadow interrupted. "If *one* cat was too heavy, *six* will sink it for sure."

"But, what can else can we do?" Twitch asked, helping Mr. Shadow get a better look.

"What if we make the raft bigger?" Tabitha shyly asked, clutching tightly to her golden chain.

"Nonsense!" Mr. Shadow barked.

"More wood! I could find more wood," Twitch added confidently.

"He's right!" Fluffy saluted. "If we add more wood, it just might work!"

"I've got a better idea!" Romeo sparkled.

"What is it?" Tabitha asked, excited.

"I can't tell you now, but I'm gonna need someone to help me." Romeo turned and looked at Fluffy. "What do you say, old buddy?" he asked with a warm smile. "Are you with me?"

Fluffy paused and remembered all the good times he'd had with Romeo. "Of course, Romeo. Of course."

Several hours later as the sun was going down, Romeo and Fluffy returned. Behind them, they dragged a large door. The words *Men's Room* were unevenly carved onto one side.

Tabitha stood up, "What's that for?" she asked confused.

"It's a door, silly," Romeo said teasingly. "It's our new raft."

Life Two

Twitch squinted his eyes and scratched his head. "But how'd you-?"

"Don't ask," Fluffy said. "It wasn't easy getting this thing down."

"Are you sure that it will float?" Mr. Shadow worried.

"It needs a little patching," Romeo said. "Now, you all get a good night's rest. You'll see, at daybreak we'll be ready to sail."

Romeo and Fluffy worked diligently all night on the new raft. Half guessing, half exhausted, and half applying all they'd learned. The two had the raft built. Like they said, it was ready by sun up.

Everyone awoke to the amazing sight of Romeo and Fluffy sitting upright on the new raft as it bobbed in the water. They sat proudly, not only because of the raft but because of their renewed ability to work together.

Tabitha rubbed her eyes happily. "I can't believe it! I can't believe it!"

"Good work, males!" Mr. Shadow applauded. "I must admit I had my doubts."

Romeo and Fluffy looked at each other and smiled.

Just like they'd learned in combat school, they had a plan. Due to his broken legs, it was decided that Mr. Shadow would be moved in the very same box used to rescue Fluffy from the pirate hole. Once they landed, he would be dragged through the city by the ropes. All attempts would be made to wake up Calvin,

Chapter Eighteen

and Twitch would return with the Sticks and taken to the Factory for some needed medical attention.

"Please, go without me," Twitch begged. "I don't want to be any trouble."

"Trouble? Trouble?" Romeo griped. "Are you kidding? It's because of *you* that we're getting out of here. Now look, we absolutely *insist* that you come with us."

They all nodded their heads in approval. Twitch sunk to the ground. "I don't know, guys...I mean..."

"What are you afraid of?" Tabitha asked. "Are you afraid people will stare at you?"

Twitch's eyes filled with tears.

"Because, if that's what you're worried about, you don't need to be," Tabitha continued. "*We* love you, and I know everyone back home will too. You're special to us. Please come home with us." She stared into his watery eyes and smiled. "Just think, you'll have good food everyday, *lots* of friends, and best of all, you'll never be lonely again." Romeo, Fluffy, and Mr. Shadow all held out a paw to Twitch. Finally, he agreed to go back to the city with them.

After a breakfast of spider webs and cocoons, everyone carefully boarded the raft. In his box, Mr. Shadow was placed on the raft by Romeo and Fluffy. Mr. Shadow screamed like a baby when the box accidentally tipped over near the water, but quickly recovered. Calvin was placed beside Mr. Shadow. Then, Tabitha, Romeo, and Fluffy followed.

Life Two

"Come on, Twitch," Tabitha smiled, looking at him with her sparkly eyes until he took his first step onto the raft.

With one paw on the island and one paw on the raft, Twitch gazed up at the beautiful statue and waved goodbye. "See ya," he said. "Don't forget to watch over us." He gave the stone lady one final look and swore she winked back at him. Easing himself onto the raft, Twitch turned to watch the sparking city before him. It had been twelve long, lonely months, and he knew it was time to go back. Maybe he'd even find Chloe, his long lost girlfriend.

With a mighty push, the raft slowly drifted away from the tiny island and began its long journey at sea. Everyone used their paws to paddle through the waves of foaming rubbish.

The mood was uplifting and cheerful as the raft floated through the water, the cats clapped and hugged and sang. Between paddling, Romeo and Tabitha danced under the gloomy haze as Mr. Shadow tapped his paw. Fluffy playfully splashed sparkles of water on his friends while Twitch dragged his can-opener in the water, slicing it through the tiny waves, dreaming of all the wondrous city sights he thought he'd never see again. Calvin snoozed through all the excitement. No one could believe this joyous moment had finally arrived. Freedom was theirs, and home was only hours away.

After about an hour, the raft began to slow

down. Everyone was tired from the rigorous paddling. One by one they stretched out their anxious bodies and stared up at the dim sky. It was a gray with stored up rain and plenty of anger. The sound of the crackling water was almost soothing, unlike the wretched sounds of Tabitha's queasy heaves over the side. Still, they drifted on wondering what life would be like back at the Factory.

"Do you think the Alleys came back?" Romeo asked as he lay with his paws crossed behind his head and his tail dragging in the water. "Do you think they've hurt anyone? If they did I'm going to line them up and skin them one by one. Then I'll pour salt on their heads and-- "

"Romeo!" Mr. Shadow barked, his nose peeking out of his box. "Stop that kind of talk!"

Romeo sat back down and de-sizzled.

"Now you know," Mr. Shadow went on, "there's a very good possibility that someone's been hurt, or worse! We should all be very cautious when we get back to the city, the *entire* city, not just the Factory."

"What do you mean, Mr. Shadow?" Tabitha asked.

"I think what he means, Tabitha," Romeo blurted, "is that the Alleys may be all over the place looking for us! Waiting to get us!"

"It is possible," Mr. Shadow said again. "Fidel knows that sooner or later we'd find a way home. He could have Alleys waiting for us at the shore with sharpened claws!"

Twitch looked at the city, then back at the island, then at the city again. "Uh," he muttered, "maybe this wasn't such a hot idea after all. Maybe we could just turn around and drop me off back at the island. It'll only take an hour or so."

"Nonsense!" Mr. Shadow protested. "We are in this together, like it or not. No one is going back! *No one!*" He scrambled around in his little confining box and pointed to the city. "If the alleys are out there, then we'll simply have to deal with them. We've done it before. We won't let all our training go to waste this time!"

Tabitha crouched next to the box and placed her head between her two front paws. "I'm scared," she whimpered, "and I just had an awful thought. It they attack us, what will Mr. Shadow do? They'll get him for sure with those two broken legs!"

"If they come for me," Mr. Shadow said calmly from the box, "then just leave me be and run for your lives. There's no sense in trying to save me. It will only cost you time and lives. I've got five more lives to go. If I have to, I can surely spare one."

Romeo peered over the edge of the box. "You're the best, Mr. Shadow," he smiled. "But don't worry, nothing's going to happen to you." A skinny, dead fish spit out of the sea and smacked him in the eye. Romeo reached to grab it, hearing his stomach growl, but it slipped out of his paws and into the dark waters.

Chapter Eighteen

Soon the rocking of the raft lulled everyone into a nap. Romeo wiggled his nose as a single drop of rain landed on it. Then, a sudden, unexpected gust of wind tossed and rattled the raft, then another gust and another. Everyone jolted up from the shock and dove to the center where it was steadier. Mr. Shadow screamed from his box as it slowly slipped toward the edge, the raft bouncing and spinning. The storm erupted over the six scared felines. The clouds dumped tremendous amounts of rain, knocking everyone to and fro. Masses of water splashed onto them crashing hard against their bodies. They clung for dear life to the ropes, digging their claws into the twine. Screams of panic wailed as the intense waves continued to thrash them up and down and side to side like a massive earthquake in the water. The little raft was surely doomed. Their hopes and dreams instantly sunk to the deepest part of the sea. Romeo spotted Mr. Shadow and his box slipping farther and farther toward the water. "Mr. Shadow!" he roared through the wind. "Hang on!"

"No, Romeo!" Mr. Shadow blared. "Stay back!"

"Never!" Romeo cried. Just then, he lunged forward to save Mr. Shadow from plunging into the violent sea. He reached for the ropes that were tied to his box but missed and slid across the slick plank. Twitch spotted him and flung himself forward. He landed on Romeo, saving him from falling off the edge. With his body firmly holding Romeo down, Twitch grabbed the flailing ropes linked to Mr. Shadow's box and tugged

Life Two

Chapter Eighteen

hard just as it was about to tumble into the rough waters. With all his might, he swung the box around sending it to the center and safest part of the raft. Beneath him, Romeo gasped for air and swallowed a huge mouthful of nasty water as it thrashed violently against his face. He passed out under Twitch. Twitch too had taken in too much water for his body to handle. He choked and gagged for the water and its yucky particles had filled his throat.

Wham! Another wave crashed onto the raft. This one larger and more fierce, nearly turning the raft on its side. The wall of water awakened Romeo and snapped him to his feet. Even Calvin finally came to, only to find himself in the midst of a horrible nightmare. Again, everyone clung to the edge praying to the almighty Bubastis with all they could. Mr. Shadow stuck his thick claws right through his box and planted them into the wood, somehow securing his place. Nobody, not even Romeo, noticed Twitch clutching his throat in agony.

"Watch out!" Tabitha warned. "Here comes another one!"

Nearly ten feet away was the terrifying sight of an enormous wave heading their way. They held on as tightly as they could. "Get down, Twitch!" Fluffy called out. "Hold onto the ropes!"

Twitch turned around, and for a split second everyone saw the immediate danger he was in. His eyes bugged out, and his mouth stuck open as the giant wave crept over his head. "Ahhhh!" Tabitha cried. "Twitch!"

Life Two

The mountain of water engulfed them in a scene of mass destruction, flinging Twitch's frail body far from the raft. "Nooo!" Fluffy wailed. Twitch's head sprung up from the water with a look of total fright. He paddled and paddled, but the waves were too strong. Out of breath, he fought as hard as he possibly could, bobbing up and down. Wave after wave thrashed over his head, tangling him farther into the sea's wrath. His two front paws flailed with exhaustion. Tabitha, Romeo, Fluffy, and Calvin struggled to stay on the raft, screaming at Twitch to swim faster, but Twitch began to swim slower, until, finally, it was over.

"Where'd he go?" Tabitha screamed over the howls. "Twitch! Twitch!"

Twitch's human nose popped up above the water, then the rest of his body. It floated there lifeless, his head completely submerged.

The storm roared for another few rocky minutes. The cats put up a strong fight, coming dangerously close to being flung off the raft and into the sea forever. Eventually, the rain and winds calmed, as did the trembling of the water. Tabitha immediately began throwing up again, and Calvin once again passed out.

Romeo and Fluffy could see Twitch's lifeless body drifting through the water like a lost fish, soggy fries stuck in his nose. He was dead. All nine lives gone. Their hearts sank as tears streamed down their faces. Everyone paused. Everyone was quiet. Then, Fluffy stepped forward and sighed, "We can't just leave him out there. That wouldn't be right."

Romeo and Mr. Shadow nodded. "Oh, Twitch!" Tabitha bawled. "Why? Why? Why did you have to be a niner?" She banged her paws against the raft and wept herself silly. Romeo pulled her close. The two of them dug into the water as fast as they could over to Twitch's body, flinging bits of debris out of their way. He was already bloated like a balloon. "We should have let him stay on the island!" Tabitha squealed. "He didn't want to come! Now look at him! He's dead!" She continued to sob hysterically against Mr. Shadow's soggy box. Mr. Shadow reached over the side of the box with his paw and gently touched her head.

Romeo carefully dragged Twitch's body onto the raft. "He just wanted another chance to be a regular cat," Romeo whispered. "That's all he wanted." He looked at the others then asked, "What do we do now? Should we take him with us to the Factory?"

"No," Mr. Shadow shook. "We've got to bury him right here. This is where he belongs." He looked up over his box at the calm blue sea that had proven so deadly only moments before. Without hesitation, Romeo and Fluffy wrapped Twitch's tainted body in a soaked sweatshirt they had taken from the island.

"I guess he was a good guy after all," Calvin sobbed.

Tabitha's eyes widened as she said with surprise, "Calvin? Is that *really* you?"

Calvin glared at her like she was crazy. "Why,

of course, it's me. Who else *would* it be?" He rolled his eyes and shook his head.

"Oh, Calvin!" Tabitha shouted. "You're back!" Calvin shook his head not certain of where he had been.

While Twitch was being properly wrapped for his burial at sea, Mr. Shadow said, "A moment of silence please."

Everyone paused and sat quietly in their thoughts. Though their time together was brief, it would hardly be forgotten. Twitch would be fondly remembered for his generosity, kindness, and bravery, crystal clear in the images he left behind. He was a cat like no other, not as much a leader as he was a giver, a *true* Stick. The painful realization that none of the other Sticks at the Factory would ever know firsthand of Twitch's courage and goodwill saddened them all the more.

Just as Romeo was about to tie the sleeves of the burial sweatshirt around the body, Tabitha caught sight of Twitch's human nose and sprung to her feet. An idea flashed in her head almost as quickly as the storm had erupted. "Wait!" she called to Romeo. "Wait just one minute."

Romeo put down the sleeves and watched as Tabitha walked up. As she did the raft tilted and rocked gently in the water. She took one long last look at Twitch as he lay so peacefully on the makeshift blanket. Carefully, she turned Twitch on his side completely revealing his human nose. She looked mournfully at that awful paper lab tag he had pierced to his nostril that he, himself, had hoped read something meaningful. Tabitha ripped it from its little metal hook.

"What are you doing?" Mr. Shadow snapped from his box.

Tabitha looked up. "Something very important, sir." Tabitha tossed Twitch's blurred tag into the water, not minding at all where it drifted. Then, she clutched her paws tightly around the golden pirate necklace which she so treasured hanging around her neck. She lifted it off her head and separated the engraved medallion from the chain. She then attached it onto the metal hook in Twitch's nose. Now he had his new tag. "He should have it."

After a long wave goodbye, Romeo tied the sleeves of the sweatshirt around the dead cat and nudged him over the side of the raft. Twitch's body floated there for a while, soaking in the salt and minerals. A few small, orange fish floated by and surrounded the body in a perfect circle. They were not there to eat him, rather it was as if they were there to protect him and carry him off into another world. Everyone watched for a moment as the fish and their friend drifted farther and farther away.

"Good bye, Twitch," Tabitha called as if he could still hear her. "Life is a treasure, after all."

Soon Romeo and Fluffy began to paddle again, continuing on their long journey home.

Chapter Nineteen

The Sticks were quiet. Everyone sat apart and dangled their paws in the water. Romeo had fun putting chunks of dead fish together like a puzzle. Tabitha watched her own barf separate in the water.

All five cats sunk into a deep and exhausted sleep. They dreamed of Mr. Sox and the Factory, Twinkle Toes, and school. Mostly they dreamed of their people, of litter, and canned food. No one dreamed of Fidel and the dogs. After his long nap, Calvin groggily came to. He licked the goo from his lips and opened his crusty lids. Then, he saw something remarkable. He rubbed his paws over and over his eyes until the picture before him became sparklingly clear. "We're here! We're here!" he cheered jumping up and down. "Everybody! Wake up! We did it! We did it!" Calvin danced around the raft, nearly shaking Mr. Shadow right out of his box.

"Just what's the meaning of all this?" Mr. Shadow grumbled. "Calvin, what are you doing?" But before he could finish his thought, he saw what had excited Calvin so. It was the cold, harsh, wonderful city only twenty feet before them. The others jolted up with matched excitement and steered the raft to the shore. A myriad of emotions swept through each and every cat, for while they all shared a new fondness for their waiting city, they equally feared it beyond their wildest imaginations.

Mr. Shadow was helped back into his box, his ropes retied and checked for security. Though the storm had dampened the cardboard, Mr. Shadow felt it had dried strong enough to survive the tugging it would endure back to the Factory. As everyone paddled the last few feet, something glistening caught Tabitha's eye. It was the SOS bottle she had sent out days earlier, floating all alone in the water. It bobbed there untouched and unanswered by feline paws. The words were blurred. The bottle cracked.

As soon as the raft reached land, the cats were off and running, liberated and free. They charged through the city like a pack of wolves, Mr. Shadow bouncing behind in his rescue box. Faster and faster they pounded, flying passed the alleyways and busy street signs. They city blew by in a blur of wavy lights and muffled sounds. It smelled as it had before, yet felt colder in a grim sort of way.

Life Two

Everyone was driven with a new sense of determination and conquest. As their paws thumped beneath their bodies, the Sticks' eyes darted around the streets in search of Alley cats and dogs. To their delight none of their grisly mugs were spotted. Then Romeo saw something. There were photographs and flyers taped to street lamps and mailboxes. Painfully curious, he slowed his stride. To his astonishment, Romeo was staring at a large picture of himself. "What are you doing, Romeo?" Fluffy roared. "We've got to keep going!"

Romeo stood still and called as loud as he could, "Stop and look at this!"

The others ran back to Romeo in a panic. "There's no time, Romeo!" Mr. Shadow screamed from his box. "We must, *must*..."

"Look!" Romeo pointed. He led everyone's eyes up to the very poster of himself. Below the unflattering picture it read in sloppy blue crayon:

REWARD FOR ROMEO
BRING HIM HOME
DENNIS CRUMB 555-8978

Chapter Nineteen

Romeo's eyes instantly went to another poster, then another and another. "Look, there's one of you, Tabitha!" he yelled. "And Darla, and Tuesday, and *Twinkle Toes*, and oh my, Mr. Sox!" Block after block, the entire city was plastered with crumpled, torn, reward photos and messages for dozens of lost or missing cats, not just Romeo and his marooned friends, but all Factory Sticks. It was an awakening moment.

"Is everyone dead? I don't understand!" Tabitha gasped clutching her tail between her legs.

"No, no, they're not dead," Mr. Shadow blurted. "It's obvious what's going on here. Hostages! They're all hostages! Quickly, to the Factory! There isn't a moment to spare!"

Like wildfire they raced passed picture after picture after picture, down each and every familiar block, over garbage piles and through the smoky sewer holes. They ran filled with passions never before felt in any cat. Fluffy clenched the ropes to Mr. Shadow's box firmly in his jaws. His fierce adrenalin pumped enough energy through his body to surge at a fast pace. Three feet behind him, Mr. Shadow and his box jolted and bounced over every crack and curb. Over and over he flopped onto his still painfully broken legs. He clung to the flimsy box with his front paws, coming dangerously close to tipping over several times.

"I see it!" squealed Calvin. "I see the Factory!"

In the distance the blurry, gray building came into sight. It was indeed the glorious Factory they

Life Two

Chapter Nineteen

had so missed and become so afraid of all in the same moment. They charged on. Soon they were only one block away. Romeo looked ahead, but he could not see Waffles or Vittles, or any Stick for that matter, guarding the building. Not a good sign. A familiar sting pinched through his stomach and held on tight. With a final leap, all the cats dashed to the front and stopped. Their chests pounded and their lungs desperately gasped for air.

At the entrance Tabitha was the first to see the stone door lying in rubble. Small lizards raced between its cracks. "What could this be?" She quivered, praying she was hallucinating.

Mr. Shadow whispered and motioned everyone into a huddle. "Something is wrong, *very wrong*," he warned. "We've got to go inside very carefully."

"But I'm scared, Mr. Shadow," Tabitha cried.

"Nonsense! Pull yourself together! Are you ready to turn back now? What about Twinkle Toes and all those posters? Did Twitch have to die just for *us* to give up?" Mr. Shadow crouched down in his box and waited for a response.

"You're right, Mr. Shadow," she nodded. "Let's do it!"

Mr. Shadow sat back up and said, "All right now, carefully, *carefully* creep into the building and don't make a sound."

"Got it!" They responded in unison.

"Remember," Mr. Shadow went on. "Keep an

Life Two

eye out for Alleys. I smell something suspicious, so be on guard. Now, let's go!"

Just like Mr. Shadow had said, everyone snuck into the Factory as slick as snails. The long hallway to the rec room was dark and mysterious and void of any candle light. The door ahead was closed, though a golden haze shone around its edges. In a huddled mass, the Sticks tiptoed up to it.

Romeo was in the front. Fluffy nudged him forward a bit, and Romeo slowly pushed it open. They stuck their noses through the crack in the door and peered in. What they saw next would stain their memories forever. Their once beautiful and elegant rec room now lay in shambles and was completely infested with Alley cats. They hung around the room like drunken sailors, drooling and cursing. They played with the Stick toys, chewed on their instruments, and peed on their books. An Alley had turned one of Lulu's paintings into a litterbox and another decorated the walls with the blood and guts of a headless mouse. Other mice were hanging from nooses.

The place looked, smelled, and felt like a horror story. At the center of all the disgust stood a mountain of puffy, fringed pillows, eight pillows high. Fidel was sprawled on the top wearing his sinister grin, picking at his stained teeth with a pencil like the almighty king he *thought* he was. His little jar of bugs glowed against his rattling collection of ID tags as he tugged mouse flesh from his teeth.

271

Chapter Nineteen

Romeo and the others became outraged. Fluffy went for the rec room.

"No!" Mr. Shadow emphasized in a whisper. But it was too late. Fluffy had lunged through the door, and although Romeo grabbed onto his hind legs, Fluffy fell face first onto the rec room floor. Romeo froze, as did Fluffy and the others.

"Intruders!" an Alley shouted.

Fidel turned his smug head and ordered, "Get them! Get them now!!"

Fidel's crew bolted from their spots and charged for the Sticks. Without thinking, Romeo and the others dodged through the rec room and headed for the back stairs, which were dangerous and weak and hardly ever used. A pack of wild Alleys followed close behind. Mr. Shadow, still in his box, remained stranded in the hallway. He hid down as low as he could, shivering and quivering himself sick.

Romeo, Fluffy, Calvin, and Tabitha reached the second floor and darted across the barren room toward the library. The Alleys pounded up the stairs close behind, Bait taking the lead. Romeo and the others ran into the library and slammed the door shut.

"Ouch!" Bait hollered, his broken tail getting caught under the door.

Inside the library Romeo, Fluffy, Calvin, and Tabitha stood close against the door with their eyes tightly closed and their breath pumping like wind. They could feel the evil Alleys pounding against the door on the other side. "Open up, *Sticks*!" Max roared. "You can't escape us this time!"

Romeo grabbed a chair from nearby and thrust it against the door beneath the handle to keep it from opening. He had seen Dennis do the very same thing when he wanted to keep his parents out of his room.

The Alleys continued to scratch and rattle the door hard on the other side.

"The Factory's our home now!" Bait yelled. "This is our territory!"

Bang! Cheeseburger hurled himself at the door like a cannon. Between heaves, he ran back to the staircase for a running start.

Inside the library, the panicked Sticks babbled nervously.

"We're dead! We're dead! We're dead!" Tabitha yelled.

"Mommy!" Calvin blubbered.

Bang! Bang! Bang! The door was practically shaken off its hinges.

Just then, as everyone fell into a state of hysterics, Romeo looked up and across the room to see a most relieving sight. "Twinkle Toes! Twinkle Toes! You're all right! Oh, thank goodness!"

Indeed, it was their lost friend Twinkle Toes. By now the others had spotted him too and momentarily forgot about the tremendous peril they were in. They ran to Toes with waving tails and beaming smiles. Romeo bounced right into his body like a rag doll and wrapped

Chapter Nineteen

his two front paws around him. "I never thought we'd see you again, Toes. You're a sight for sore eyes."

However, despite the tearful reunion, Twinkle Toes stood still, like a stone statue. Romeo looked into his blank stare. "Twinkle?" he asked. "What's wrong? What's happened to you?"

"Later," Fluffy hurried. "We've got to get him out of here. We've got to get *ourselves* out of here!"

"Come on, Toes!" Romeo scrambled. He tugged on his friend's ears, swinging his head back and forth, but Twinkle still didn't move. He just stared straight ahead.

A cry from behind a large, fallen table caught everyone's attention. Romeo crept up to it and peered over the edge. To his horror he saw twenty Sticks all huddled on the floor, tied up with ropes and bandages like prisoners. Even Waffles and Vittles were there.

"Oh my!" Romeo cried in shock. "Mr. Sox! Uncle Fred! Maybelle! What the?" Romeo turned to Twinkle for help.

"Get away from him, Romeo," Mr. Sox warned, motioning to Twinkle Toes. "He's one of *them* now!"

Twinkle Toes walked up to Romeo and stared him down with eyes of steel. "The name's *Jailbird*, see?" Twinkle said grimly. "Jailbird. Got it?"

"What? You've gone crazy!" Romeo growled. "You're not Jailbird! You're Twinkle Toes, one of my best friends!"

"It's true! It's true!" Snickers yelled from his

restraints. "They've brainwashed him and put him on the nip! Romeo, you and the others get out of here while you still can!"

Romeo heard a sudden hiss and turned around to find Twinkle Toes glaring at him with a vicious scowl. His eyes glowed yellow, piercing Romeo to the core. Just then, the door flung open with a boom spilling a myriad of Alleys into the library. Romeo and his raft crew barreled through the room right past the classroom and back around again to the far staircase. Jailbird and the rest of the Alleys sped behind them, leaving the hostages helplessly alone to wallow in their misery.

As Romeo, Fluffy, Calvin, and Tabitha zipped up the dusty stairs, they passed more and more Sticks tied up just like the others. Heartbreaking though it was, they pressed on until they felt they could go no farther, finally reaching the forbidden fifth floor with its dark reminders of the damaging fire. With Jailbird in the lead, the Alleys also reached the fifth level and met the Sticks face to face.

Trapped, Romeo, Fluffy, Calvin, and Tabitha took a few slow steps backwards across the creaky floor. Jailbird stared into their eyes, looking more and more sinister by the second. His back was arched high, and a slow hiss escaped his mouth. "Come on, Toes," Romeo pleaded. "It's me, Romeo. You remember, don't you? We're pals. Buddies."

But it was no use. Jailbird had fallen under

275

Chapter Nineteen

Fidel's nasty spell. He was a changed cat. He came closer and closer as the four Sticks slipped farther and farther toward a large, broken window behind them. With not a moment to spare, Fluffy got an idea he simply couldn't afford to ignore. With a thunderous roar, he bolted forward leaping onto Jailbird. Caught off guard, Jailbird bounced up with a shrieking cry sending Fluffy directly into Romeo and the others like a bowling ball. Romeo, Fluffy, Calvin, and sweet Tabitha all stumbled and lost their balance, wobbling closer and closer to the window.

In a final, fatal blow, Jailbird lunged forward with such brute force he scared all four Sticks right out of the window. Flailing and screaming, they plummeted down the five stories, the wet wind beating against their contorted faces. With a sickening thud, they landed on the hard, cold, concrete sidewalk splashing a wave of puddle water all over their broken bodies. Blood seeped from their noses and mouths and mixed with the rain, creating a river of red.

Each and every one of them lay dead, bones crushed and dreams dashed all at the unthinkable paws of a former Stick, a former friend. Five floors up Jailbird smirked as he peered out the shattered window. Fluffy, Calvin, and Tabitha were on the sidewalk in a jumbled heap. Then, Jailbird spotted Romeo's lifeless body a short distance away. He was on his side, blood running from his ears. Jailbird puffed with pride. He and the Alleys had won. Fidel's

Life Two

precious Romeo was dead...again.

Back in the rec room, Jailbird and the other Alleys immediately informed Fidel of the good news. He was still perched high atop his throne of pillows plucking the tail off a live mouse. Dangling above his head was Mr. Shadow in his box. It was attached to a beam with the ropes from the island. The box rocked and swayed as the beam creaked and moaned. Mr. Shadow trembled inside his cage like a frail little kitten, fearing for his lives and his friends. His legs ached and swelled even more, for neither one of the Alleys that tied him up so savagely showed any mercy for his injuries. None of his hissing or screaming did a bit of good. Unaware that his four island heroes were lying dead outside, Mr. Shadow swung helplessly, imprisoned like a rat. He peeked over the side of the box and listened to Twinkle Toes' shivering tale about what had happened on the fifth floor. He was horrified. *No, Twinkle Toes! No!* he screamed silently in his head. *There's no hope now. There's no hope now.*

"Good work, males," Fidel congratulated. He looked at Bait and grinned. "Two of Romeo's lives down, *seven* more to go!" Fidel stuck out his ragged claw and patted Jailbird on the head.

Jailbird sat beside his master and purred.